41 Tips for Success in Share Market

41 Tips for Success in Share Market

Mahesh Chandra Kaushik

Published by
PRABHAT PRAKASHAN PVT. LTD.
4/19 Asaf Ali Road,
New Delhi-110 002 (INDIA)
e-mail: prabhatbooks@gmail.com

ISBN 978-93-5322-705-0
41 TIPS FOR SUCCESS IN SHARE MARKET
by Shri Mahesh Chandra Kaushik

Edition
2024

Paperback Price
₹ 250.00 (Rupees Two Hundred Fifty only)

Printed at
Narula Printers, Delhi

This book is dedicated to
my 71,000 followers in the stock market who,
with their faith and affection,
have inspired me to spare time out
of my very busy schedule
and pen 41 trading tips for them
so that none of the small investors
who read this book,
do not lose money in the stock market.

Preface

I entered stock market trading in the year 2005. I was then just an amateur investor like other common investors. However, I knew only one mantra that one should treat every job as God's work and execute the same just like worshipping God.

Hence, I always believe that I am not trading for myself. That Almighty has assigned this job to me and I have to execute the same successfully.

That very inspiration and faith always helped me learn from my mistakes and I started my blog 'Share Genius' in the year 2009 to share my experiences. When common people started reading and appreciating my blog, I was filled with deep inspiration, motivation and energy and I hardly noticed how quickly the number of followers of my blog and YouTube channel grew to 71,000 within no time.

Securities and Exchange Board of India (SEBI) made its (Research Analysts) Regulations effective from the year 2014; accordingly, nobody is permitted to provide stock market tips through blog or YouTube channel without first registering with SEBI and passing the Research Analyst examination conducted by NISM. Hence, respecting the government regulations and complying with the same,

I announced closure of my blog and YouTube channel. Reacting to this, many of my followers sent me e-mails and advised me to clear the Research Analyst examination and get registered with SEBI. I would not then need to close my blog and channel and even people reaping benefits from the free tips that I have been providing as a service right from the year 2009, would not be deprived of the same.

Thus, I transitioned from a common investor like you to a registered research analyst. While writing this book, I assume this to be my responsibility to train all its readers in such a way that none of the readers fails in a stock market.

Before reading this book, please keep this in mind very clearly that 'investing' and 'trading' in a stock market are entirely separate activities. This book has been written from the point of view of making money by trading and not investing; you should, hence, read the same with that very frame of mind.

You may share your experiences with me through email on my id: mahesh2073@yahoo.com.

—Mahesh Chander Kaushik
Research Analyst
J. J. Colony, Pindwara-307022
Dist. Sirohi, Rajasthan

Mobile No.: Please excuse me for not providing my mobile number here, as, with so many followers, it would not be possible for me to talk to you all on mobile. However, you may always contact me through e-mail. I will try my best to respond to those e-mails as much as possible.

E-mail: mahesh2073@yahoo.com

Thanks

I am indebted to my Sadgurudev Shri Shri Satyanarayanji Falahari Baba, Sarneshwar Mahadeo Mandir, Lotana for the spiritual energy provided to me for writing this book.

Before writing this book for 'Prabhat Prakashan', all my books were self-published books on Amazon, i.e., this is my first book written for any specific publisher and I feel a sense of honour for the same.

I am also sincerely thankful to my wife Smt. Seema Kaushik, who never stopped me from taking risks in the stock market. It was her support for my investment decisions and her nature not to discourage me even for my wrong trade decisions that helped me continue in the stock market for a long time and come out as a successful trader.

— Mahesh Chander Kaushik

Contents

1

Make Sure to Formulate Strategy before Trading

When you see a magnificent building, do you realise that the building design would have been prepared on paper before starting construction? Or, do you assume that some masons would have just come and straightaway started constructing the building with bricks and mortar in a random way and building got erected just like that?

No building is constructed without preparing its design first.

For a moment, let's assume you are a captain in the army. What would you do if you have to win a battle? Would you start fighting after preparing a strategy or would you just instruct the soldiers to go ahead and start fighting and you would think over later how to fight?

You might have heard this story. Long ago, there was a highly successful businessman. He had four sons. When he grew old, he handed over one rupee to each of them and told them, "Go and use this one rupee for a business and earn profits. I will hand over management of my business to the one who can successfully earn a profit of two rupees from this one rupee."

That businessman wanted to check who among his sons actually had the business acumen, as most of the people are gamblers and not businessmen, and they do not even know the basic principle of trading that trading has to be done with some strategy. A gambler just jumps in and thinks only later on about formulating a strategy.

Thus, my first trading tip for you is—make sure to formulate a strategy before trading in stock market. Well, the kind or nature of strategy would be discussed in forthcoming trading tips.

□

2

Grow a Small Plant into a Big Banyan Tree

Have you ever watched a plant germinating? Have you seen a banyan tree and a banyan seed in your life? The banyan seed is as small as a mustard seed. Can this grow into a full-grown banyan tree in a single day?

Of course not! The banyan seed first germinates into a small pretty sprout. Next day, the same grows further a bit. Gradually, that small soft sprout grows into two leaves. Those small reddish leaves look so pretty. Nature is trying to teach you trading through the same. It's a different matter however, if you are really interested to learn from the same!

There is no place for hurry in Nature. That banyan plant keeps growing gradually. Within a few years, this becomes capable of providing shelter to birds. After few more years, this becomes capable of providing shade to travellers. And very soon this turns into a huge banyan tree. Would you prefer to create a trading strategy somewhat similar to that where the business of your trading develops like a banyan tree? Or, would you like to make some good money out of one to seven exciting trades and then, after losing all your money, run away from stock market and curse the same for the rest of your life?

You must have by now understood my second tip of the day. You should invest a small amount for your first trade, just like a banyan seed. Gradually, as you keep making profits, you should keep increasing your trading amount accordingly.

Let me explain this in detail. Suppose you have a capital of ₹5 lakhs. You want to use that money for trading in stock market and earn a large profit that would be enough to generate a monthly income of 40 to 50 thousand of rupees. Then, you just need to start trading with a sum of ₹10,000 only. Have an aim in your mind—'If I am able to make a profit of ₹2,000 with this ₹10,000, i.e., if I am able to convert my investment of ₹10,000 into ₹12,000, I would increase my working capital used for trading to ₹20,000, just like a banyan tree. When I earn a profit of ₹4,000, I would increase the working capital to ₹30,000. When I earn a profit of ₹6,000, I would increase the same to ₹40,000.' Thus, for every ₹2,000 made as profit, the working capital may be increased by ₹10,000.

You may say, "What if I am not able to make profit?"

As such, I do not believe you would suffer loss in trading if you go through this book fully. You can surely make profit. It is also not so difficult to make money in the stock market with disciplined trading. On the contrary, it is easier to make money from trading as compared to investing, as you may be able to earn on your investments only in a bull market, whereas trading provides earning opportunities in both bull and bear markets.

Even otherwise, you don't need to invest your entire 10,000 rupees in a single stock. You are reading a book from Mahesh Kaushik and I can't see my readers losing. I never advise you to invest your entire money in a single trade transaction. We would trade by dividing that amount into 10 smaller parts. After all, how small is that banyan seed that grows into a plant! Similarly, in order to grow like a banyan tree, we also would have to start with trades in smaller lots and then, as soon as we earn a net profit of ₹2,000, we would increase our capital to ₹20,000. This way, we would have ₹22,000 for trading—₹20,000 from our base capital and ₹2,000 from our profits.

Here, I am repeatedly referring to 'net profit', as a business generally involves both profit and loss. Incurring loss is not a bad thing for a business. Actually, an endeavour cannot be called a business if it does not involve any kind of loss. And a businessman is regarded as successful when profits in his business exceed losses. 'Net profit' here refers to the amount left after adjusting all the losses against all the profits, and you have to increase your capital only when you earn a net profit' of ₹2,000.

Thus, the second tip of the day is—start your trade with 1/50th of your total capital and keep on increasing your working capital with 1/50th of original capital every time you earn 20% 'net profit', thus growing your trading business like a banyan tree.

□

3

Make Small Trades Only

Your broker generally provides you facility to make trades in intraday trading with a very small margin, i.e., if you make two trades—buy at a margin and sell with an appropriate 'stop loss'—simultaneously, the broker assumes that your loss is limited because of your 'stop loss'. Hence, he provides you facility to buy-sell stocks for amounts anywhere between 50,000 and one lakh rupees with a margin of just ₹1,000. This is referred to as 'margin plus' or similar names.

Most of the new traders lose their money because of this only. Why so?

Have you ever got caught in a traffic jam? You would have noticed that small vehicles like bicycles and motorcycles are able to weave through the jam, but heavier vehicles like truck can't.

In the same way, you also would get caught in the jam just like that truck if you make trades of that size in the market.

This happens because this is a market. A 'buy' trade for a specific quantity of stock would get executed only when a seller is available with the matching quantity of that stock. Similarly, a 'sell' trade for a stock would get executed only when a buyer is available for the matching quantity of the same stock.

Have a look at the following snap. I am just showing you the market depth for TCS stocks as displayed on NSE website.

Tata Consultancy Services Limited

Get Derivatives Quote | Option Chain

Series: EQ |

Symbol: TCS ISIN: INE467B01029 Status: Listed

Market Tracker

2,362.35	Pr. Close	Open	High	Low	Close
▼ -88.35 -3.61%	2,450.70	2,384.90	2,385.00	2,355.10	-

Trade Snapshot | Company Information | Peer Comparison | Historical Data

Print

VWAP	2,372.94
Face Value	1.00
Traded Volume (shares)	14,75,248
Traded Value (lacs)	35,006.75
Free Float Market Cap(Crs)	1,25,305.85
52 week high	2,839.70 (07-OCT-14)
52 week low	1,995.00 (13-DEC-13)
Lower Price Band	2,205.65
Upper Price Band	2,695.75

Order Book | Intra-day Chart | Stock V/s Index Chart | Quarterly Charts

Buy Qty.	Buy Price	Sell Price	Sell Qty.
5	2,362.15	2,362.35	9
127	2,362.00	2,362.60	48
99	2,361.95	2,362.65	10
1	2,361.90	2,362.75	47
12	2,361.70	2,362.95	25
93,723	Total Quantity		69,912

+ Security-wise Delivery Position (12DEC2014)

+ Value at Risk (VaR in %)

You may observe that market price of the stock is ₹2,362.35. Look at the order book—somebody is ready to buy 5 stocks at ₹2,362.15 per stock. On the other side, 9 stocks are available for sale at ₹2,362.35 per stock. Suppose you place an order to buy 100 stocks in intraday trading using a good amount of margin. You may assume that you are buying at ₹2,362.35, but when your trade gets executed, you would get 9 stocks at ₹2,362.35 and 48 stocks at ₹2,362.60—the rate indicated for the next seller above. Next 10 stocks would be bought at ₹2,362.65. Thus, the price of the stock would go up because of your order itself, and when you sell this big lot, your sale order itself would result in the stock price going down. This is just an example for TCS that is a large-cap and liquid stock. Thus, your order brings a change in stock price by some 40 to 50 paise. If you place a single buy order of 2 to 3 lakhs of rupees for a low-volume stock, that itself may take the stock to upper circuit; and when you sell the same lot, stock price would just crash.

You may get surprised to observe all this. You received stocks at prices higher than the price at which you had placed the 'buy' order, and your stocks got sold at prices lower than the price at which you had placed 'sell' order, and you incurred a good amount of loss.

You may think you could have placed a 'limit' order instead of a 'market' order. But, in that case, your order may not get executed if no seller or buyer could be found selling or buying at the 'limit' rate quoted by you.

Hence, you should not buy or sell stocks on margin for more than 40 to 50 thousand of rupees in a single trade, using minimum brokerage charges from your broker. Do check the market depth of a stock before selecting the same for trade. Selected stock should be a high volume stock so that sellers or buyers are always available for your 'buy' and 'sell' orders; else, you may end up buying stocks at prices close to upper circuit and selling at prices close to lower circuit. Even 'stop loss' does not work here as in the case of a low-volume stock, buyers and sellers are generally not available at your quoted 'stop loss' price.

Thus, here is my third tip—use small trades to earn small profits.

It takes drop by drop to fill a pitcher. If you make a profit of 200 to 500 rupees in a single trade and if 7 out of your 10 trades in a day are profitable, you end up making a profit of 2,000 to 2,500 rupees; but you should make only small trades.

□

4

Always Keep Your Profit Target Small and Keep Stop-Loss Still Smaller

As I have already advised, you should start your intraday trading business with a capital of ₹10,000 and then gradually increase that capital. Suppose you do not increase your capital and make a profit of only 2% in a month. That means, you earn ₹200 only after doing intraday trading for a month, and next month, with this ₹10,200, you again earn 2% profit, i.e., ₹204 and your capital grows to ₹10,404.

As above, if you keep earning a profit of 2% every month and you keep on adding your profits to your capital, can you tell me what would be your capital after 30 years?

You may have a heart attack when you hear the answer. Hence, people with feeble heart should avoid reading further! Earning a profit of just 2% every month as above, your capital of ₹10,000 would grow to ₹1,24,75,611 (Rupees one crore twenty four lakh seventy five thousand six hundred and eleven only) in 30 years!

Those who do not believe this may refer to the copy of excel sheet containing this calculation, provided at the end of this book as Appendix A.

Is it really a big target to make a profit of ₹200 in a month with a capital of ₹10,000? There are around 20 trading sessions in a month. That means you just need to make a profit of ₹10 everyday!

Can there be a businessman who is not able to earn ₹10 even after investing a capital of ₹10,000? A vegetable vendor is generally cleverer than a novice stock trader, as he brings vegetables worth ₹10,000 everyday and makes 200 to 300 rupees profit by selling them, whereas even when I give a target of ₹10 only to a stock trader, he ends up losing 200 to 300 rupees of his capital by the end of the day.

This is the reason I always say—one who does not know how to sell tomatoes cannot sell stocks, as selling tomatoes and selling stocks have a lot of similarities. Tomatoes, if not sold on time, may get rotten. If they are not sold even with some loss, the entire lot of tomatoes may get spoiled. The tomato trader is aware of this fact. He makes sizeable profits on fresh tomatoes. As dusk approaches, he starts lowering his profit target, and before the tomatoes go rotten, he sells them even incurring some loss. But a novice stock trader sticks to a fixed target and waits for the stocks to go rotten. And, in the end, he exits only after incurring a big loss.

A tomato trader sells his tomatoes even with a meagre profit of one rupee, but a novice stock trader loses even his small profits in the hope of making 5% to 20% profit in intraday trade, and, finally, his stocks go in loss.

Thus, the tip no. 4 has this very message—do not keep your profit target more than 1% in intraday trading.

If you make an intraday trade of ₹10,000 for a stock, paying a margin of ₹1,000 to ₹2,000 only, you may make a profit of 1%, i.e., ₹100 out of the same, whereas your earning target for the day was only ₹10. If you have made 100 rupees, you have achieved the target for 10 days, and that means, at that speed, you may grow your ₹10,000 to ₹1,24,75,540 in 3 years itself, instead of 30 years.

But, the main problem that is encountered here is that you do not book your profit of ₹100 and you even do not use stop-loss. That results in this profit getting wiped out and your trade finally makes you lose 200 to 300 rupees instead of earning 100 rupees. And then you forget about profits and start trading to cover your losses.

In this reference, I recall an advice given by a spiritual teacher. He says, "If you do not stop making mistakes, even Lord Brahma would not be able to impart you supreme knowledge. The only eligibility to receive supreme knowledge is to stop making mistakes."

Thus, in order to make profits in trades, it is necessary to keep a small target of 1% for profits and even smaller target of 1/2% for stop-loss.

That means if your profit target is 100 rupees and your trade is already in a loss of 50 rupees, your tomatoes have started to get rotten. You may secure your capital only by booking that loss of 50 rupees, and you may still end up with profits by the end of the day.

This very point would be discussed in the next tip.

□

5

Ratio between Profit and Stop-Loss Must Be 2:1

Let's repeat the last portion of the previous tip.

You have a target to earn ₹100 and your trade is showing a loss of ₹50, i.e., your tomatoes in the form of stocks are getting rotten. You can secure your capital only by booking this loss of ₹50 and you may still end up with profit instead of loss by the end of the day.

But, how could that booking of loss of 50 rupees turn into a profit?

It is essential to keep the ratio between profit and loss in stocks as 2:1 to ultimately make profits.

As you know, whatever precaution you take to select stocks, there is no system that can guarantee 100% success in trades. Your trades may end up in loss, and this does happen.

Let's assume you maintain a ratio of 2:1 between profit and loss in this business and enter into 10 trades during a day. As you are aware, you may use a margin of ₹1,000 to ₹2,000 for creating a trade of ₹10,000. Thus, with your capital of ₹10,000, you may enter into 4 to 6 trades at a time and later, when margins are released after booking profit or loss for some trades, you may use that margin again for fresh trades. According to me, with margin money of ₹10,000, you may be able to make about 10 trades of ₹10,000 each during a day.

Suppose you keep a profit target of 1%, and use stop-loss of 1/2%, and out of 10 trades, you lose in 6 trades and make money only in 4 trades. Thus, you earned ₹100 each in 4 trades, i.e., a total of ₹400, and lost ₹50 each in other 6 trades, i.e., a total of ₹300. You are still making a profit of ₹100. That means, even with 4 trades out of 10 going successful, you end up making profit. Even after deducting brokerage and other expenses from that profit, you are left with ₹10; you are ultimately earning and not losing.

However, greed and fear instincts overwhelm a new trader. He does not book loss as per stop-loss even when his trade is down by 1/2%. In fact, he does not even apply stop-loss thinking that his stock would go up again, and his loss ultimately grows to 4% to 5%.

Similarly, he does not book profit when stock price goes up by 1% as his greed prompts him to wait for still higher profit of 4% to 5%.

With all this, even if 7 out of his 10 trades go successful, he ends up making net loss, as he would have earned some 2,000 rupees from those 7 undisciplined trades, but would have lost 2,500 to 3,000 rupees in the rest 3 trades because of his indiscipline. As a net result, he loses 500 to 1,000 rupees out of his capital. Next day, his greed goes up further to recover this loss and finally ends losing still more.

Thus, if you have to make money, it is very necessary to keep a ratio of 2:1 between profit target and stop-loss.

This principle is used by successful traders all across the globe. If you feel 1% profit and 1/2% stop-loss are too low, you may increase them at most to 2% profit and 1% stop-loss. However, in my opinion, if you enter into trades after properly analysing the charts and picking stocks with good movements, it is quite easy and fast to realise profits of 1% instead of 2%. This also facilitates release of margin that may be used for fresh trades.

It is an essential condition to maintain a ratio of 2:1 between profit target and stop-loss in order to make money in stock trading. If you do not want to use stop-loss, you should take up swing trades for short periods instead of intraday trades. Process of swing trades has been discussed in detail in subsequent chapters in this book. Even with swing trades, you may easily earn 2-5% on your capital every month, without incurring losses.

□

6

Trade Only in Stocks Having Large Volumes

NSE website provides a list of stocks that are quite active in the current session, i.e., the stocks running into large volumes.

You should also move with the crowd. The prices of stocks that are being traded in high volumes are either going to rise sharply or going to decline badly. Trading in such stocks may be beneficial for you in the sense that the price of your stock would not encounter sharp fluctuations as both buyers and sellers would be available in great numbers, and, hence, there is very less chance of your stop-loss getting triggered.

Also, for trading in such stocks, normally referred to as liquid stocks, the brokers generally have lower margin requirements. For example, for a midcap stock with low volume, your broker may block 3-4 thousands of rupees for a 'buy' or 'sell' trade of ₹10,000, whereas, for a high volume large-cap stock, you may initiate a trade of ₹10,000 with just ₹800 to ₹1,600 as margin.

Margin amounts are not fixed. This is decided based on liquidity of the stock. Hence, stocks having large volumes only should be selected for trading. I would advise that you pick your stocks from high-volume stocks of the previous trading day, as that enhances your success rate. You may download previous day's rates copy in Excel format from NSE website and you may pick up stocks with the largest volumes for that day from that list.

There is yet another way for the same. You go to 'Live Market' link on NSE website and select 'Most Active Securities' option. That displays the most active securities for the current session. You may pick your stocks from that list. For your benefit, I am giving below a screenshot of the relevant page. Please have a look carefully to understand which link you need to select.

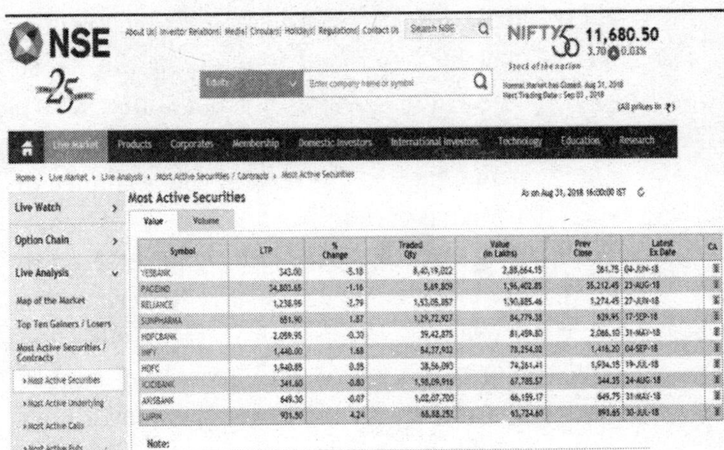

Symbol	LTP	% Change	Traded Qty	Value (in Lakhs)	Prev Close	Latest Ex Date	CA
YESBANK	343.00	-5.18	8,40,19,022	2,88,664.15	361.75	04-JUN-18	
PAGEIND	34,803.65	-1.16	5,69,809	1,96,402.85	35,212.45	23-AUG-18	
RELIANCE	1,238.95	-2.79	1,53,05,857	1,90,885.46	1,274.45	27-JUN-18	
SUNPHARMA	651.90	1.87	1,29,72,927	84,779.38	639.95	17-SEP-18	
HDFCBANK	2,059.95	-0.30	39,42,875	81,459.80	2,066.10	31-MAY-18	
INFY	1,440.00	1.68	54,37,932	78,254.02	1,416.20	04-SEP-18	
HDFC	1,940.85	0.35	38,56,093	74,261.41	1,934.15	19-JUL-18	
ICICIBANK	341.60	-0.83	1,98,09,916	67,785.57	344.35	24-AUG-18	
AXISBANK	649.30	-0.07	1,02,07,700	66,159.17	649.75	31-MAY-18	
LUPIN	931.50	4.24	68,88,252	63,724.60	893.65	30-JUL-18	

Notes:

But, how do you know which stock is going to rise and which one is going to fall. This would be discussed later in this book.

Remember the tip of the day—you have to trade today in stocks that had the largest volumes the previous day. Those who had bought stocks on the previous day expecting profits may sell today resulting in fall in price and you may earn by short-selling. Also, if any stock was traded on the previous day based on some expectation and that expectation is still alive today, the price of the same may go up further and you may earn profit by taking a long position.

□

7

There is no Good Stock or Bad Stock; it is Either a Loser or a Gainer

You have learnt in the last six tips that you can start trading in the stock market even with a small capital and, maintaining an appropriate ratio between profit and stop-loss, you have to earn profits by entering into multiple trades, as there is no perfect system available where you can predict the outcome of a trade with 100% accuracy. But if you maintain a ratio of 2:1 between profit and stop-loss, you may make money even with 7 losing and 5 profit-making trades out of 12 trades. For example, for trades each having value of ₹10,000, if your profit target is ₹100 and stop-loss target is ₹50, you would incur a total loss of ₹350 for 7 loss-making trades and make a profit of ₹500 for other 5 trades, thus earning a net profit of ₹150.

And, as you are not a novice trader, it is very unlikely that 7 out of 12 trades go wrong. In fact, just the opposite happens in reality. 6-7 trades out of 12 may result in profits and 5-6 trades may go wrong; this is normal. This happens even with large traders and that is the reason stop-loss has been devised.

I had read a book by Nicolas Darvas titled 'How I Made $2,000,000 in the Stock Market'. He has impressed upon just one point—there is no good stock or bad stock. There are only two types of stocks in the market—one, the stocks gaining and other, the stocks losing. Hence, you just need to identify them. That would help you make money in trading.

As such, there are plenty of applications/systems already available to help you identify losing and gaining stocks. There are many indicators like R.S.I. on Candlestick Charts for this purpose; however, before we discuss these systems in detail, I would like to tell you in my subsequent tips about the system that I use to identify gaining and losing stocks.

□

8

Do Not Mix Different Segments of Trading

There are five separate segments or divisions for trading and investments in the stock market. Generally, a new trader is not able to make a clear demarcation among them and treat all those five segments as a single domain. This leads them to failure in both trading and investment.

These five segments are as follows:

1. Intraday trading or Margin trading
2. Swing trade or Buy Today Sell Tomorrow (BTST)
3. Trading in Futures or Derivatives
4. Trading in Options
5. Delivery Based Trade in cash

In fact, if you buy or sell (*You may borrow stocks from broker and sell and then buy and return the same before the end of the day. This is called 'short selling'. This kind of trading is done when there is a likelihood of the price of stock going down*) stocks in intraday at opening of the market and book you profit or loss before close of the market the same evening by selling or buying (in case you have gone for short selling) those stocks, this segment of trading is called Intraday Trade or Margin Trade.

In the case of a Swing Trade or BTST, the period for which you hold the stocks may range from 2-3 days to even 30 days; that means you do not have to close positions the same day as required in Intraday Trade. If the position is closed on next trading day, it is termed as Buy Today Sell Tomorrow (BTST). But it is not necessary to go for BTST. And the trades where period of holding may range from one day to one month are called Swing Trades. This involves holding stocks for periods more than that required for Intraday and less than that required for Delivery Based Trade in Cash.

In the case of a 'Trade in Futures or Derivatives', only an agreement to buy or sell stocks on a particular future date is executed instead of investing directly in stocks. That date is called 'Expiry'. This period may be 7 days (e.g., Bank Nifty) and 30 days (e.g., Nifty and other stocks). Here, the stocks have to be bought in lots and one lot may be valued at even 5 to 10 lakhs of rupees. Facilities for trading on margin are available here also.

Option is a kind of insurance. Here you enter into an agreement to buy/sell stocks on a particular date and then pay premium for the same. On the designated date, if your buy or sell transaction results in gain of more than the premium amount, you are in profit, and if your gain is less than the premium amount, you incur loss. Options are safer compared to Futures in the sense that your loss is limited to the amount paid towards premium.

The fifth kind of trade is Delivery Based Trade in Cash. In this trade, you pay in full for the stocks and take physical delivery of the same into your Demat account. There are two kinds of trade here also—short-term trade when you sell your stocks before end of one year and long-term trade when you sell after holding for one year or more.

Hence, this tip simply means that you should not mix the above five segments. Let's take an example. Rohit takes a position of ₹10,000 in intraday. He plans to book his profit or loss before close of the market. He has to pay a margin of ₹1,500 for this position. The trade, however, goes into a loss of ₹60, but Rohit does not close his position. He expects the stock price to go up. By the end of the day, that loss goes up to ₹350, but Rohit is still not ready to accept the same and feels that the price would surely go up the next day. Why to take a loss of ₹350 unnecessarily? In place of a margin of ₹1,500, he pays the entire ₹10,000 as margin to the broker and changes his intraday position to delivery.

As delivery would take 2-3 days, Rohit wants to sell them before delivery using BTST trade or Swing trade. But, it's a disappointing day again and his loss goes up to ₹730. Rohit still takes it lightly and plans to sell the stock the next day. The stock price goes up the next day, but still his loss is not covered. His loss comes down to ₹240. Rohit believes the price is showing an upward trend and he decides to take delivery and wait for some time before booking profit through short-term trading.

But the stock goes down again. Rohit is now looking at a loss of ₹1,200. From a short-term investor, he now shifts to a long-term investor. He wants to somehow make a profit from this transaction, even if he has to hold the stock for a year or so.

Such kinds of investors hold their loss-making stocks even up to 4-5 years.

What did you observe in the above example of Rohit? Rohit shifted from Intraday to BTST, then to Cash, then again to short-term and, finally, to long-term investment. This was wrong. Mixing these different segments this way is definitely a wrong step.

As it has been explained in earlier tips in this book, if you are doing intraday trade, you must close your position if your loss touches 1/2% or book profit if you have made 1% profit. In such a case, while taking an intraday position of ₹10,000, Rohit should have applied stop-loss of 1/2%, i.e., ₹50. After booking this loss of ₹50, he could have got his margin released and used the same margin for a fresh intraday position of ₹10,000. He could have earned a profit of 1%, i.e., ₹100 from that position and after squaring off his loss, he would have been still in profit for the day. He could have even used that margin for a third position.

Thus, the main point of this tip is that you should maintain clear demarcation among different segments of stock market and decide on your target, stop-loss and time frame before taking a trade position.

In the author's opinion, you should go for Swing trade in place of Intraday trade and preferably trade in Options instead of trading in Futures. This would reduce the possibility of loss and increase chances of profit. Swing trade and Options trade would be discussed in detail in the subsequent chapters.

□

9

Keep Your Greed and Fear under Control

An English trader has written in his book that a human is by nature an unsuccessful trader as greed and fear are his natural instincts.

Hence, just as a training in army makes a person a soldier, a study and training in science creates a scientist, trading in stock market is also an art that can be leant only with constant practice and control on emotions.

In fact, greed and fear are two such emotions that may turn you into an unsuccessful trader. Let's see how?

When you are in a profitable trade position, you may get consumed with the desire for more profit; but suddenly the profit starts getting wiped out. You then consider it right to wait for some more time, but the profit gets wiped out too fast and your profit-making position turns into loss. You are still under greed and decide not to apply stop-loss. The trade finally turns into a sizeable loss.

When you take a trade position next time, the emotion of fear overtakes you. The moment you find the position making a small profit, you decide to book the same, as you fear that even that small profit would get wiped out.

Possibly, that trade could have given you a much better profit.

It was for the purpose of teaching you how to control these very emotions that you were advised in previous tips to keep a target of 1% for profit and apply stop-loss of 1/2% for your trades.

When you are able to take yourself to a winning position during the day, you may raise your profit target and stop-loss. Assume that you enter into trades of ₹10,000 each and keep a target of ₹100 for profit and ₹50 for loss. Fortunately, out of your first 7 trades, 5 trades are successful and you make ₹500 from them and you lose ₹100 from the other 2 trades. You are, thus, having a net profit of ₹400. In such a case, even if you take fresh positions with higher profit target of 2% and stop-loss of 1%, there is no chance of your making loss at the end.

Thus, in general, keep control on your greed and fear and maintain a ratio of 2:1 between profit and stop-loss. Initially, trade with low profit targets and still lower stop-loss. Once you have made good profit, you may gradually enhance your profit target and stop-loss for that day in such a way that by the end of the day, you do not end up wiping out your entire profit of the day.

□

10

Do Not Average Out Falling Position in Intraday

Here is a story to help you understand this tip.

A lady vegetable vendor buys a basket of okra and sits down to sell the same to retail customers. But there is very little demand for okra that day in the market. Also, a big trader has just received a large consignment of okra in a truck. She had bought okra at the rate of ₹60 per kg and wanted to make some profit by selling the same at ₹65 per kg. But that big vegetable trader is selling okra @ ₹50 per kg only.

Now, should that lady vendor buy one more basket of okra @ ₹50 per kg in the hope that the average cost of the two baskets of okra would come down to ₹55 per kg and when that big trader runs out of stock, she would be able to sell her stock at ₹60 per kg?

If your answer is 'Yes', it is wrong because, just as intraday position needs to be squared off before close of the market in the evening, the vegetables of that lady vendor would get spoiled if not sold by the end of the day. There is no guarantee that the big trader would be out of stock before the end of the day as supply has been more than the demand on that day.

Hence, that lady vendor does not do that, as she can observe that her one basket of okra is anyway going to be spoiled, and even if she buys one more basket of okra, what is the guarantee that the big trader would sell all his stock by evening and rates would go up again, considering that there is already oversupply of okra in the market? On the contrary, her loss may go up further, as the big trader would further reduce his rate to ₹40 per kg by evening when his stock of okra starts getting spoiled.

A barely literate vegetable vendor knows how to do business. She does not try to average out her stock of vegetables that is not getting sold by buying fresh stocks. However, when a stock trader buys a stock and his position goes into red, his ego gets hurt. He believes that the tip that he has received from a renowned research analyst can't go wrong and he makes fresh purchases at reducing prices to average out his position. But, when the price does not go up even by evening, he incurs two-fold loss and starts cursing the research analyst, and again gets into a never-ending search for a perfect tip. Tips from any research analyst can never be 100% successful. If you have to trade in stocks, the only way to be successful is—do not average out your falling position in intraday trade; apply stop-loss and maintain a ratio of 1:2 between loss and profit.

Though, in the case of a Swing trade, where position is held for 1 to 30 days, it is permitted to continually average out a falling position following some defined rules. There, we keep revising down our profit target with every average out action.

This kind of Swing trade would be discussed in detail in the subsequent chapters of this book. For the time being, just keep in mind—if your position in an intraday trade is going into red instead of earning profit, it is better to get out of the position than trying to average out the same. In our above example, the lady vendor sold her stock of okra at a loss before the prices went further down and before the stock got rotten, thus saving herself from still worse losses, and used that money to buy fresh vegetables and earn profits to recover her above loss.

In fact, even in intraday trade, profits may be earned sometimes by averaging out positions, as stock market is quite unpredictable. For some traders sometimes, the proverb 'a blind man acquiring a quail' is proven valid, but most of the times, attempts of averaging out intraday positions result in increase in losses. Hence, it is necessary to keep your sense of ego as well as your emotions like greed and fear away while going for stock trading. It is wrong to nurse egos like—I am not wrong, so and so gentleman can never be wrong or I will somehow make a profit from this very trade, etc.

Decide your profit target and stop-loss before you enter into a trade and then follow the same rigidly. Do a business like a business; do not treat the same as a question of win or loss like a cricket match.

Practical Exercise

Find out a trader who has incurred a huge loss in intraday trade. Just ask him whether he had tried to average out his falling position.

You will find that in almost all cases, his answer would be 'Yes'.

□

11

Which is the Best Indicator for Trading?

I keep on receiving, on daily basis, several emails, YouTube comments and Blog comments requesting me to give lessons in analysis of technical charts and provide information on the best indicator on a technical chart for trading.

There are more than 200 indicators like RSI, VWAP, IMI, EMA, DMA and SMA on technical charts to analyse stock movements in the stock market. Some of them are quite simple, whereas some are very complex.

All the traders keep on looking for the best indicator out of them. Generally, a new trader is always trying to get hold of an indicator that would work like Aladdin's lamp and provide him 100% success.

They go through many new books on stock market in search of that best indicator. It is possible that you have also bought this book with the aim of quenching your thirst for that perfect signal. There are lakhs of books available on intraday trading and analysis of technical charts. All of them provide extensive lessons on trading by mixing 1-2 or 3-4 signals; but when a new trader, after reading such a book, tries to test those lessons in real world, he finds that the suggested system is also not perfect.

He starts his search again. There are millions of videos on this subject on YouTube. After viewing them, you may feel that you have found a perfect trading system. That system may help you gain in real trading for a few days. And then you incur heavy losses to the extent that even after applying stop-loss in your trades, your entire profit gets wiped out.

The best indicator that I am now going to tell you is somewhat bitter and difficult to digest. Definitely, a new trader is not able to digest this; but this is an eternal truth. The sooner you assimilate the same, the longer you may stay in the market. The eternal truth of this best indicator is that 'there is no system perfect for intraday trading in the stock market'.

What do we do then?

Nothing! You have to just keep in mind that instead of searching for a 100% perfect system, you just need to take small positions using your own system, whichever way you feel you may have better chances of succeeding in your trade, and try to earn profits maintaining the ratio of 2:1 between profit and loss, as has been explained in earlier tips.

As such, in my personal opinion, an indicator of a breakout from VWAP is most accurate. This will be discussed in detail under Tip No. 15.

Practical Exercise

Buy the stocks that are being shown as oversold on 14-day RSI chart, for intraday positions, and sell those stocks that are being shown as overbought on that chart. You may observe that this policy results in successful positions in most of the cases, but not always. Sometimes stocks are shown as oversold or overbought on the chart, but you end up losing instead of making profits in your trades based on the same.

That simply means that technical indicators are not always correct, and hence, it is not advisable to lose your hard-earned money through small stop-losses in trades based on such indicators. You will have to either turn into a full-time trader and stay focussed on the trading screen or shift to swing trade today or tomorrow.

In the next tip, you would come to know why an indicator going correct most of the time in intraday trading fails right at the time you take a trade position.

□

12

Beware, Somebody is Watching Your Trade

It is said that walls also have ears! Nowadays, when trading is performed using computer systems, your intraday position can be easily viewed on the screen of your online trading service provider. Even you may easily watch orders currently available in the market on the market depth screen.

Thus, the position you have taken, whether you have taken margin position or cash and carry position, all this can definitely be watched by your online trading service provider. In addition to that, it is difficult to say who all like your broker, sub-broker, trading member and others may also watch your position; and in this computer age, it's not impossible also.

You may be thinking how does it affect you even if somebody is able to see your order or your trading position?

Have you ever played cards?

Do you allow other players to see your cards?

How does it affect you in that card game when some opponent players are able to see your cards?

I, the author of this book, am not 100% sure who all may be able to watch your intraday or margin position and what are the possibilities of the same being misused.

However, if there is even 1% possibility of the same, you are in danger. My wife had even received a phone call from one of the online trading platforms. Some lady was saying, "Seemaji, I am observing that you generally keep a very small stop-loss that gets triggered quite often." When I asked who she was, she said, "I am trading manager for Seemaji." I asked her, "What right have you got to watch our position and stop-loss details?"

She explained, "My company has appointed relationship managers for each and every customer so that we may guide our customers in making money from trading. Seemaji's trading id has been assigned to me and, hence, I am able to view all her trades, profit bookings or loss bookings and stop-loss."

Now, suppose you have bought on margin 1,000 stocks of Reliance at the rate of ₹1,043 per stock. Now you keep a target of ₹1,048 and stop-loss at ₹1,038. A big operator is watching your position. He knows what all orders are there in the market at different rates. He can see that your stop-loss will be hit if he sells his 5,000 stocks, as, when he sells 5,000 stocks at a time, the rate would gradually fall from 1,043 and would reach a level of ₹1,035 soon and your stop-loss of ₹1,038 would be hit. At that very moment, he would also buy 5,000 stocks back.

Thus, his 5,000 stocks were sold at rates ranging from ₹1,043 to ₹1,035. Many of the traders like you would like to close their positions bearing this loss. Thus, he would buy 5,000 stocks from them on rates ranging from 1,035 to 1,038 and earn a good profit. You would incur a loss of ₹5,000 at the rate of ₹5 per stock because of your stop-loss getting hit.

Practical Exercise

Look for a low-volume stock in the market. Watch its market depth. I have told you about market depth under tip no. 3. The market depths that you watch on NSE and BSE websites are generally not real-time. They may have a lag of few seconds, but market depth can be watched in almost real-time on trading platforms like Zerodha-Kite.

Suppose, the stock price is currently at ₹16.10 and you are able to see following orders in market-depth:

Buy Orders

16.10	-	500 stocks
16.05	-	1 stock
16.00	-	5 stocks
15.95	-	8 stocks
15.90	-	1,000 stocks

Sale Orders

16.15	-	503 stocks
16.20	-	10 stocks
16.25	-	15 stocks
16.30	-	88 stocks
16.35	-	58 stocks

To perform this exercise, you have to ensure that volume is low and the orders are standing still for quite some time. Now, if you have enough funds to buy @ ₹16.35 all the 674 stocks (503+10+15+88+58) available for sale at rates ranging from ₹16.15 to ₹16.35, i.e., if you have ₹16,500 available as margin, you may just place an order to buy 1,000 stocks at market price and watch. You would observe that all the above sale orders get triggered and the market price of the stock goes up to somewhere around ₹16.45.

Thus, the stock price can be brought up and down with the help of any big order and, that's how, big traders may trigger your stop-loss in just a minute.

Please be warned here that while doing this exercise, some big trader may go faster than you and bring the price down again in seconds by selling their stocks, resulting in a loss for you. Hence, you should take up this exercise only when you have enough capital, you have the capacity to bear the loss in case you suffer a loss and you should select a stock that has a very low volume.

□

13

Go for BTST or Swing Trade in Place of Intraday

If you, instead of going for intraday trade on margin, buy stocks with 'Cash and Carry' option and sell them the next day, the trade is called 'Buy Today Sell Tomorrow'. That only is referred to as BTST in short. When stocks are sold after holding them for 2 to 30 days, it is called 'Swing Trade'.

It was just BTST before introduction of intraday trade. A position in swing trade increases possibility of profit for you, as, firstly the operator can't manipulate to trigger your leverage position and, secondly, you get more time during which the stock may perform better.

It may be a losing proposition to average out in an intraday trade, but in the case of a swing trade, if you average out in a disciplined way following specified rules and keep on revising down your profit target with every average out action, you may be able to easily exit without incurring any loss.

As delivery of stocks is taken in the case of a swing trade, it is treated as investment instead of trade. Even under tax regulations, instead of treating this income as speculative income, it is treated as short-term capital gains that you may save through income tax harvesting. Details of income tax harvesting would be discussed in subsequent tips.

I will discuss 'Sharegenius' system for winning swing trade in the next chapter.

□

14

Sharegenius System for Winning Swing Trade

For a stock traded at an exchange, the average price for all trades done on a particular trading day is called 'Volume Weighted Average Price (VWAP)' for that day.

Suppose the Volume Weighted Average Price of TCS stock is ₹1,948.30 for 17 October, 2018. In that case, you should place an after-market order or limit order to buy 1 stock at this average price of ₹1,948.30, so that on 18 October, 2018, the next trading day, that 1 stock is purchased for you if the price reaches VWAP of the previous day.

I have inferred based on my analysis of past data that there is more than 90-95% possibility of your getting the stock at Volume Weighted Average Price of the previous trading day.

This way you are buying only one stock per day at VWAP of the previous day. You should use this method of trading only if you are maintaining your trading account with some discount broker where there is no brokerage for delivery (cash) purchases and where only one or two rupees are charged towards GST and STT for a purchase of ₹1,000.

You just keep buying one stock everyday. As soon as you get a profit of 2.5% on the average price of all stocks that you have bought till date, you sell and exit. However, you should use this method only for 50 NIFTY stocks or 30 SENSEX stocks. Even when these 50 NIFTY stocks or 30 SENSEX stocks keep falling continuously for a few days, they do bounce back at most within a month or two, and do provide opportunity for 2.5% return.

Let me explain this in more detail. If you buy one stock daily for any of the 50 NIFTY or 30 SENSEX stocks at VWAP of the previous day, you very soon get a chance to book 2.5% to 3% return on average price of all stocks bought—sometimes in 4-5 days, sometimes in 6-7 days and sometimes in 10-20 days. If market goes into a bear phase, this time may go up to 30 to 60 days.

In a normal market, 2.5% return can be achieved in 4 to 20 days.

There is also an advanced version of this method. In that, you place order for 4 stocks, instead of one stock, on daily basis—first, at VWAP of the previous day, second, at 1% less than that VWAP, third, at the previous day's low and fourth at 1% less than that previous day's low. Suppose you have placed such 4 orders for TCS stocks. When market goes down, all 4 orders would get executed. When market goes up, at least one stock at the previous day's VWAP definitely gets bought; sometimes even two stocks get bought. Whenever you find a profit of 2.5% to 0.5% over average price of stocks bought, you should book the same and exit.

Here, you should keep lowering your profit target as per the average price. For example, if after first day's purchases, you are able to get 2.5% profit, you should book the same immediately. However, if you do not get that profit target and you bought more stocks following the same method, you should book profit even if you get 2% over average price of stocks bought.

If you have averaged out for three consecutive days, you should exit even with a profit target of 1.5%. You would be secured in this way and as you get back your capital, you would be able to enter into fresh trades even with a small capital.

If, unfortunately, you are not able to get the expected return even after averaging out for four days, you should revise your target to 1% only.

On the fifth day of the week, that is also the last trading day of the week, if you are not able to achieve the profit target even after averaging out following the above method, you should take even 0.5% profit. As I have indicated above, in the case of brokers like Zerodha, there is a delivery charge of around ₹16 while selling any quantity of stocks, and for buying or selling 2,000 stocks, there is a cost of around ₹4 towards sundry items. Hence, even after selling with just 0.5% profit, you would be able to exit with some small net profit after adjusting the above expenses. Next week, you may start the process again with profit target of 2.5% and as the stock price had been continuously falling for the last 5 days, the possibility of a bounce-back and achieving that 2.5% target goes up considerably for the week ahead. The *funda* here is that by following the above method of trading and booking varying levels of profit, sometimes 2.5%, sometimes 2%, sometimes 1.5%, sometimes 1% and sometimes just 0.5%, you may achieve an average weekly return of 1% quite comfortably, without incurring any losses.

□

15

VWAP Breakout Method

Even if you trade in intraday, you may trade at breakouts from VWAP. For this, you just keep a watch on VWAP of the day and the price of the stock. If the stock price is above VWAP of that day, wait for the price to come down.

The moment the situation reverses, i.e., the stock trading above VWAP suddenly comes down, you should take a short position. You may observe that in most of the cases, when a stock trading at rates above VWAP of the day comes down, it does fall further by another 0.5% to 1%. Though, on trading days with wide fluctuations, the stock may quickly rise back and, hence, instead of being greedy, you should book even a 0.5% return the moment you get the same.

Similarly, if the stock is trading below the VWAP of the day, wait for the same to go up. If the stock trading below VWAP suddenly goes up, you should take a long position immediately.

You would observe that in most of the cases, when a stock trading below VWAP of the day goes up, it does rise further by another 0.5% to 1%. Though, on trading days with wide fluctuations, the stock may quickly fall again and, hence, instead of being greedy, you should book even a 0.5% return the moment you get the same.

This method is successful in 60 to 80 percent of cases and, hence, even this is not 100% perfect. But, trading is an art and this is an important part of that art.

You may keep stop-loss, etc., in the same way as advised in earlier tips, i.e., the ratio between stop-loss and profit should be maintained at 1:2.

In my experience, the possibility of loss goes up when we use stop-loss, as small stop-losses get triggered by rapid fluctuations in price. What should you do then? Trading without a stop-loss may result in a much bigger loss for you.

I have found a solution for the same. You should use either small trade method for stop-loss or time-bound stop-loss. These are discussed in the next tip.

□

16

Small Trade Method for Stop-Loss

A trader enters into a trade of ₹25,000 and sets a stop-loss of ₹250, i.e., 1% of trade amount. His profit target is ₹500.

If 4 such cases of stop-loss are hit, he incurs a loss of ₹1,000.

Now, let's see our small trade method for stop-loss for a comparative study.

Instead of a position of ₹25,000, he may go for margin trade with ₹500 and focus on exit with 1% profit without applying any stop-loss. With his margin of ₹500, he may take a position of ₹2,500 and then use VWAP breakout method detailed under Tip No. 15, to make a profit of 1%, i.e., ₹25. What could be the maximum loss that he may incur in this case? Assuming that he did not set any stop-loss, he may incur a loss of up to ₹500, i.e., his margin money, only if the stock price falls by 20%.

Firstly, if you are trading in stocks belonging to indexes like NIFTY, the chances of their prices falling together by 20% in a single session is almost nil. Secondly, even if the price does go down, the maximum loss of ₹500 is, in a way, stop-loss only.

Thirdly, you should apply a time-bound stop-loss instead of applying the same in percentage. Thus, if you are taking a position on Volume Weighted Average Price (VWAP) breakout, you should keep the position small and decide in your mind that you would wait for a maximum period of 20 minutes to take profit and if you do not get the same, you would exit with whatever loss it results into.

Here, the loss on account of 20 minutes' limit is your stop-loss, and if the breakout is real, an appropriate profit is most likely to be achieved within those 20 minutes.

As has been explained earlier, it's not bad to lose in some of your intraday trades. You have to just ensure that your profits always exceed your losses.

Practical Exercise

Before going for real trades, you should try to make imaginary trades based on the above method and keep record of the same on paper. If you see profit within 20 minutes, just make a note of the same. If the trade is going in loss, keep record of the loss incurred. Try this exercise for at least 5 days and then review the results. Please do let me know about your results through comments on my YouTube channel or blog.

□

17

Control Over Mentality of Leverage Trading

As I have advised you earlier, taking a large position under influence of your greed may be dangerous for your financial health.

A very large position on margin is called 'leverage position'. Any contrary movement in the market may result in a huge loss to you. Suppose a trader has an amount of ₹100 for margin. As per rules, he should use a maximum amount of ₹25 as margin for one position. But, if the trader is able to make a good profit from the same, he gets influenced by greed and thinks of using the entire margin amount of ₹100 for a position to earn bigger profits.

This very greed proves to be a curse for him. Hence, you should always maintain a ratio of 4:1 between your margin and position. You would have heard of the ratio between profit and stop-loss till now, but perhaps you are coming across a ratio between margin and position for the first time.

Let me explain this ratio in detail. Suppose, you open an intraday trading account and deposit ₹40,000 into the same as margin money. Most of the new traders, in such a case, keep on taking positions until they consume the entire margin money. For example, they take a position in a stock with ₹4,000 margin. They take next position using ₹5,000 as margin. Like that, they keep on taking positions in different stocks until they end up using entire ₹40,000 as margin.

These very positions are leverage positions, i.e., such positions that consume your entire margin money are called leverage positions. Now, let's understand how a big portion of your capital may get wiped out if you do not use stop-loss or even when your stop-loss is not hit.

Let's assume you took leverage positions and also set your stop-loss. Now, if there is some major movement in the market, your broker would ask for extra margin to maintain your positions and you do not have any margin money left in your account. In such a case, because of shortage of margin, your broker would book loss closing all your leverage positions and you would have to incur a huge loss.

Whereas, as per my rules, if you have ₹40,000 as margin, you need to maintain a ratio of 4:1 between margin and position, i.e., for a total margin of 4 rupees, you can take positions of up to one rupee only. Here, as you have ₹40,000 as margin, you should retain ₹30,000 in your account and take intraday trade positions with ₹10,000 only. Always remember that the market is going to open next day also. We are not here to become a millionaire in a day. As per this rule, you can use only ₹10,000 as margin for intraday trades on that day, not more than that. The balance amount is for the next day and you must keep in mind that this money is NOT to be used for margin the same day under any circumstances. If you feel so, you may even swear by God or swear by any of your dear ones not to get influenced by greed and ensure maintenance of a ratio of 4:1 between margin and positions.

This rule would save you from getting overwhelmed by emotions. If you use ₹10,000 as margin and end up losing ₹2,000 that day in your trades, you would be left with a margin of ₹38,000 only. In that case, as per 4:1 rule, you should take positions with ₹9,500 margin only, being 1/4th of ₹38,000. Similarly, if you make a profit of ₹2,000 on the first day with ₹10,000 margin, you would have ₹42,000 as margin for next day and then you may use a maximum of ₹10,500 margin for positions the next day.

This way, following this 4:1 rule for margin, you may save yourself from taking leverage positions by getting swayed by emotions. You might have heard many a times that many traders lose their entire capital in intraday trade on a single day. This happens only because of leverage positions and trader's audacity to fight the market.

I will discuss about fighting the market in the next tip.

□

18

Do Not Fight the Market

A trader should be free from the emotions of greed, fear and ego. You would have to trade like a robot to become a successful trader. Do not mix emotions with your trade. You may be wondering now as to why I have started preaching so much!

You would be able to understand my lesson after going through the story of Lalit Prajapat. Lalit Prajapat had discovered a marvellous way of trading. In fact, getting used to shooting in the dark, he thought of a strategy—'let me treat previous day's close price of a stock as base, and I would not take any position till the time stock remains above that base price, but the moment it comes below that previous day's close price, I would take a short position.'

He actually did the same thing. He selected four stocks. Out of the four, he got chances in three stocks where, after moving above previous day's close prices for some time, the stocks started falling below those prices. Lalit took short positions the moment their prices came below previous day's close prices, and he made good amount of money as stocks fell further down.

Next day, Lalit attempted the same strategy with double the margin money. For stocks that started below previous day's close prices, he kept on taking 'buy' positions the moment they moved above their close prices, and similarly, for stocks that were moving above their previous day's close prices, he kept on taking 'sell' positions the moment they fell below their close prices. He made good profit that second day also.

Now, on the third day, he increased his margin money further and followed the same process. But, market was quite volatile that day, i.e., the market did not move in the same direction; instead, it fell first and then went up fast. Thus, when he took short positions for stocks that had moved below previous day's close prices after hovering above those prices, the stocks moved up with double the speed after some time and they closed also at higher levels. Mr. Lalit had to suffer a good amount of loss.

Now, Lalit felt—'my method was not wrong (this is what is called the sense of ego). I just did not set stop-loss. I should surely take a short position when a stock goes below previous close price, but I would set a stop-loss of previous close price just in case the stock moves up again.'

But, how to recover the loss incurred in such positions? Lalit thought over the same and took a decision—'if after falling below previous close, the stock starts moving up again, I would close my short position at previous close price and take a long position ('buy' position) for double the quantity. The double profit that I make from this position would be enough to set off my above loss from stop-loss and still provide me some earning (this was the sense of greed).'

Next day, he chose the stock A. Its previous close price was ₹340.80. The stock opened at ₹342.40. After trading for some time, it came below ₹340.80 to ₹340.70. Lalitji followed his method and sold 100 stocks. The price fell down further to ₹337, but he did not book profit. He thought, "Now that the stock has fallen that much, where is the chance of its going up? Let it fall further and increase my profit (the emotion of greed)." But, just the reverse happened. After a short time, the stock shot upwards and from ₹340.70, it went up to ₹341.30. Lalitji booked loss in his short position at ₹341.30 and bought 200 stocks (i.e., took a long position for double the quantity). After going up, the stock suddenly went down. He had not set any stop-loss for this position and the stock came down to ₹336. Now, he got swayed by fear. He immediately sold 600 stocks in place of 200 stocks. This covered his long position of 200 stocks and created a short position for 400 stocks. Before he could set a stop-loss for the same, the stock came back to ₹341. Now, Lalitji started fighting the market. If the price of the stock fell, he would short for double the quantity and if the price went up, he would buy four times the quantity. And, fighting like that, he could not even notice that he had incurred a sizeable loss on the day marred by wide fluctuations.

It is possible that many of the traders, who have lost money fighting the market, may find this story to be their own, but this may happen with anybody after getting swayed by emotions.

Thus, the lesson of the day is—do not frequently change your strategy on the same day to fight the market. Just remember that none of the strategies is 100% correct. If you could not make money in the market on a day, just keep in mind that the market is going to open again the next day.

Keep your stop-loss and profit target fixed. Keep control over your ego, greed, fear and anger.

□

19

Do Not Mix Intraday Trading and Long-Term Investment

If you buy a stock for investment and the same starts giving a profit of 5% to 6% on the same day or after 1-2 days, you sell the same thinking that you would buy the same back when the price comes down again. But, it's not possible every time. Hence, never mix day trading with long-term investment. Keep your capital segregated into day trading, short-term investment and long-term investment segments, and do not mix them.

As far as my advice is concerned, I feel the swing trade method may be more beneficial for you as compared to both intraday trading and long-term investment.

If swing trade is done in good bluechip stocks and you are able to generate an average return of 2% per month from the same, you may earn 26.82% in a year calculating the return based on compound rate. Whereas, it is possible that even though you selected a good stock for long-term investment, the same may not perform well during that year and you may not be able to make any money, instead your stock may even go in loss. However, under swing trade (details of which are discussed later), your return for three years, calculated at compound rate, may go up to 103.99% if you are able to manage 2% return on a monthly basis. You can understand that there is no guarantee of your stock selected for long-term investment going up by 103.99% in three years, whereas, even if you earn half of your target in your swing trades, you would definitely earn at least 50% in three years.

Do not get worried, the entire process of swing trade would be explained in subsequent tips.

□

20

Observe Market Trend and Then Trade

There is a saying in the stock market—'The trend is your friend', meaning that it is always helpful to observe the market trend and trade along with the same, just as it is easy to swim in a river in the direction of the current, but it is very difficult and sometimes even impossible to swim against the current.

If you guess the trend on the start of any trading day by simply checking if NIFTY and SENSEX are in green or red, you may be proven wrong.

For this, as per my method, you should not enter into any trade during the first one hour after opening of the market. Then, note down the high and low of SENSEX or NIFTY during that one hour. Check the level of index at current time, i.e., one hour after opening of the market. If the same is near the high reached during the first hour of the market on that day, the market is in an uptrend on the day. If the level of index after one hour is near the low of that day, market is in a downtrend.

Naturally, if the market is in an uptrend, you should take more of buy positions on that day and if the market is in a downtrend, you should take more of sell positions.

For example, if the last close for NIFTY is 10,648.50 and when market opens at 9:15 in the morning, it opens in red at 10,599.70 and even around 10:15 am, this is at 10,620.40, i.e., 28.10 less than the previous close, most of the traders in the market treat this as a downtrend only; but this is your mistake.

As per my method, if after opening at 10,599.70, NIFTY touched a high of 10,630.20 until around 10:15 am and it was at 10,620.40 around 10 am, when compared with high and low of the day, it was nearer to the high of the day and, hence, the market was in an uptrend that day and whatever bad news was there had been discounted already. In such a situation, you are sure to get caught if you go for short-selling. You should take long positions in such circumstances.

Thus, decide on the ratio between your long and short positions for a trading session after looking at the market trend of the day.

□

21
Observe the Stock Trend and Then Invest

Just as the method of finding out the market trend has been explained in the last tip, you should observe the stock trend also and then make investments. The process is the same as explained in the previous tip.

First of all, let the price of the stock settle down for the first 60 to 80 minutes. Then compare its price against high and low of the price on that day. If the stock price is closer to the high reached till that time on that day, the stock is in an uptrend. It must be remembered in this regard that it does not make a difference even if the price is below previous day's close and is in red. If the stock price is near the high reached during the first 60 minutes, it is treated to be in an uptrend only.

Though, you need to keep this in mind that this method also provides just a guess.

The success rate may be higher here but this can't be 100% precise. As has been explained in previous tips, none of your methods can be 100% effective in intraday trading, as a competing trader may watch your position in market depth and use much larger capital to take a position opposite to your position and demolish any of your trading strategies in a minute. If you have started reading this book from the middle, you may read Tip No. 12 again to get more details in this regard.

Hence, this is my advice again that swing trading is a more effective method than intraday trading and if you can earn from swing trading much more than what you may earn from intraday trading, why should you be bothered of leverage intraday trading on margin at all?

□

22

Adopt VWAP Method of Swing Trade

VWAP has already been discussed in previous tips. In VWAP method of swing trade, you have to use one stock out of NIFTY 50 stocks day-wise on each of the five trading days of the week.

Let me give an example of the method followed by my wife. She has picked following stocks from NIFTY 50, one for each of the five days of a week.

Yes Bank on	xxxday
IOC on	xxxday
NTPC on	xxxday
ONGC on	xxxday
Tata Motors on	xxxday.

In order to maintain privacy, I have mentioned as 'xxxday' instead of providing actual names of the days, as I do not want everybody to start taking up swing trade together for the same stock on the same day; that may raise demand for that stock on that specific day and it is possible that you do not get the stock on that day on previous day's VWAP. And then you would complain that you are not getting stocks even after following my method!

She invests a specific amount (we will explain in the next tip what would be this amount) everyday in these identified stocks.

Let's assume Tuesday is fixed for IOC. She would look into VWAP of Monday for this stock after closure of the market, i.e., the average price of all the stocks of IOC traded on that day—this is available on NSE website. Those who still have problem may watch my video on YouTube and learn about VWAP, or you may also have a look inside the black ellipse on the screen-shot below.

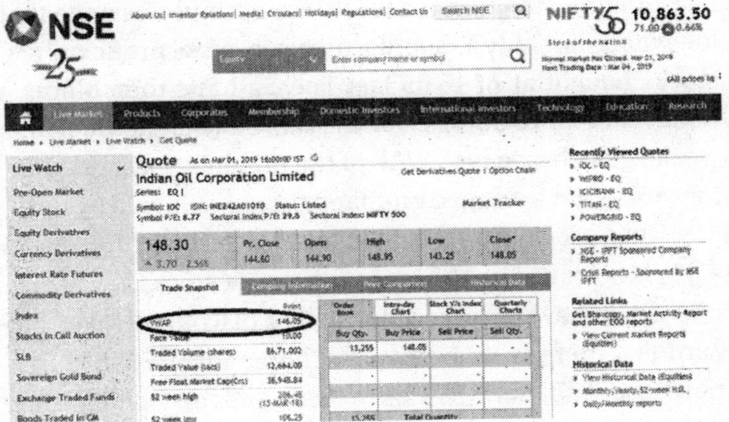

Here, VWAP of previous day (after close of market) for IOC is ₹146.05. Now, whatever amount (let's assume this to be ₹2,000) she has decided to invest in this would be divided by the VWAP, i.e., ₹2,000/₹146.05 = 13.69 rounded off to 14. She would then place a limit order (after market order) before opening of the market for next trading, for purchase of 14 stocks of IOC at ₹146.05. When the market opens the next day, 14 stocks of IOC would get bought as per her order whenever the price comes to ₹146.05 or below any time during the day.

In this method, the probability of VWAP of the previous day being hit on the next day is almost 90%. This way she buys stocks of the five selected bluechip companies on five days of the week for specified amount and if she gets profit of 4.5% (after adjusting all expenses like brokerage, short-term capital gains, STT, delivery charge, etc.) on any stock any day during the week, she books the same and exits.

Otherwise, she repeats the same process the next week. If IOC stock has been continuously falling, this results in averaging out once in a week. For example, assume that for whole last week, she did not get 4.5% profit on IOC stocks bought at ₹146.05 last Tuesday. She then places a limit order for IOC stocks for the same day of the week this week again, based on VWAP of the previous day and, thus, the stocks get averaged on that price.

This process is repeated until a return of 0.5% to 4.5% is achieved on the average price of stocks.

If you have your account with a discount broker like Zerodha, there is no brokerage charge for 'Cash & Carry' purchase and only STT is levied, and on selling, only around ₹16 is charged towards delivery. I will tell you how to set the target for swing trade in subsequent tips.

Do not get amazed to see the profit target being mentioned as '0.5% to 4.5%' for subsequent weeks. As I have explained in previous tips also, as you go on averaging out your purchases, you have to keep reducing your profit target also by 0.5%. This would be discussed in detail later.

□

23

How Much to Invest in a Single Stock in Swing Trade?

If you select 5 large cap (NIFTY 50) stocks for swing trade and you have total capital of ₹25,000 for investment, you should invest ₹1,000 for each stock every week. That means that you would be investing ₹5,000 in one week having five trading sessions, and even if the market continues to fall for five weeks (though this generally does not happen and a bounce-back of 4.5% to 0.5% is definitely seen in between), you would still be having sufficient funds for investment.

Now, what if you want to start swing trade with a capital of ₹50,000 instead of ₹25,000? Or, what should you do when you start with ₹25,000 as capital and the same grows to double, i.e., ₹50,000 after some time?

(You have been told about the power of compound interest earlier in Tip No. 4 as to how, with only a 2% compound monthly return, an amount of ₹10,000 may grow to a sum of over ₹1.24 crores in 30 years. Thus, even with an average monthly return of 2% only, it does not take much time for ₹25,000 to grow to ₹50,000.)

Thus, if you have to start swing trade with a capital of ₹50,000, you should not increase your investment amount of ₹1,000 in five stocks to ₹2,000 each. Instead, you should now invest ₹1,000 in one stock of NIFTY 50 on each day of the week as above and select one more stock from NIFTY Midcap 50 for each day and invest ₹1,000 in the same at previous day's VWAP.

For example, on Monday, you invest ₹1,000 in a NIFTY 50 stock and another ₹1,000 in a NIFTY Midcap stock.

Similarly, on Tuesday, you invest ₹1,000 in another NIFTY 50 stock and ₹1,000 in another NIFTY Midcap stock, and so on.

If your capital is ₹75,000 or grows to ₹75,000, you may even include 5 small cap stocks from BSE Small Cap Index stocks. For example, you may go on investing ₹1,000 in a NIFTY stock, ₹1,000 in NIFTY Midcap stock and ₹1,000 in BSE Small Cap stock, i.e., ₹3,000 on each day of the week, taking stocks from different companies on different days, and if you do not get 4.5% return during that whole week, you may average out the stocks next week on the designated days of the week.

Thus, you would be investing ₹15,000 per week at the rate of ₹3,000 per day, and as per the rule, you should do this investment only if you have capital equivalent to five times your weekly investment, i.e., 15,000 x 5 = 75,000. This way, you would be able to continue doing 'average out' even if you do not get target return for five consecutive weeks.

What if our capital is ₹1,00,000?

You may invest ₹2,000 in one NIFTY stock, ₹1,000 in one NIFTY Midcap stock and ₹1,000 in NIFTY Small Cap stock—totalling ₹4,000 everyday and ₹20,000 for the entire week.

The entire capital is not required to be deposited into trading account in one go. For example, if I take positions for ₹20,000 in a week as per the above method, I would check every Sunday the balance available in my trading account. Suppose, there is an amount of ₹7,200 left in my account. In that case, I would transfer ₹13,800 to this account to make the balance as ₹20,000, and I would review position again next week. If I am able to book profits in some stocks during the week on achieving target returns, and the balance in my trading account goes above ₹20,000, I would withdraw the excess amount; if the balance remains short, I would transfer the required amount.

What if the available capital is ₹1,25,000?

The investment pattern per day would be ₹2,000 in one NIFTY stock, ₹2,000 in one NIFTY midcap stock and ₹1,000 in one small cap stock—totalling ₹5,000. Thus, the ratio of your daily investment amount to your capital would be 1:25 so that you would have enough capital even if you do not get your target return in any of your stocks for 25 consecutive trading sessions.

If your capital is ₹1,50,000, you may invest ₹2,000 for each of the three stocks, i.e., ₹6,000 per day.

If your capital is ₹1,75,000, you may invest ₹3,000 in NIFTY stock and ₹2,000 each for other two stocks, i.e., ₹7,000 per day. I hope you would have understood by now what ratio has to be maintained between daily investment amount and your capital.

After you get a situation of ₹5,000—₹5,000—₹5,000 per stock, i.e., your capital is ₹3,75,000, you should increase the number of stocks by one instead of increasing investment amount per stock.

Thus, if you have a capital of ₹4 lakhs, you should take two NIFTY stocks instead of one, and invest ₹3,000 for each of the two NIFTY stocks, ₹5,000 for midcap stock and ₹5,000 for small cap stock everyday. Similarly, with still higher capital, you may invest in two midcap stocks.

Starting with ₹25,000, you have to move ahead in a disciplined way as above. In the next tip, you would learn how to set profit target in this process.

□

24

Determination of Profit Targets

Here, I would use an account with Zerodha as an example for determination of profit targets. If you have your trading account with any other brokerage firm or charges increase in future, you may adjust your targets accordingly.

First of all, let me set forth the target rates and later I would discuss the target and profit.

S. No.	Stock Average Out at Volume Weighted Average Price	Profit Target (%)
1.	Target for the week when stock bought first time	4.5
2.	Target for second week at average price after averaging out	4
3.	Target for third week at average price after averaging out	3.5
4.	Target for fourth week at average price after averaging out	3

S. No.	Stock Average Out at Volume Weighted Average Price	Profit Target (%)
5.	Target for fifth week at average price after averaging out	2.5
6.	Target for sixth week at average price after averaging out	2
7.	Target for seventh week at average price after averaging out	1.5
8.	Target for eighth week at average price after averaging out	1
9.	Target for ninth week or any week after that at average price after averaging out	0.5

Let me explain this in more detail. Suppose, you have a capital of ₹25,000 and you buy stocks for ₹1,000 using Zerodha account as per the process detailed in the last tip. There is no brokerage (as at the time of writing this book) applicable at the time of purchase and only STT and GST amounting to a total of around one rupee is charged. Similarly, when the stock is sold, ₹16 is charged towards delivery charge and another one rupee towards taxes. Thus, buying (with delivery in cash and carry) and selling stocks for ₹1,000 costs in total around ₹20 that includes 15% short-term capital gains tax (income tax) on profit.

Though, you may also save this short-term capital gains tax. This would be discussed under income tax harvesting tip later.

If you book a profit of 4.5% on ₹1,000, i.e., ₹45, you get only around ₹25 as your profit that comes to around 2.5% net return.

Similarly, after averaging out next week, if you book profit of 4% on your investment of ₹2,000, ₹30 would have to be reduced towards charges (delivery charge of around ₹16 is charged every time irrespective of the quantity of stock—whether you sell one stock or 1,000 stocks). Thus, out of 4% of ₹2,000, i.e., ₹80, if you deduct ₹30 towards costs, you are left with ₹50, that is, 2.5% net return. In the same way, if you book 3.5% profit on ₹3,000, you would get ₹105 and after deducting around ₹40 towards costs, you would be left with ₹75 as net profit.

Taking the same forward, even for an investment amount of ₹4,000, booking a profit of 3% would provide you a net return of around 2.5% after adjusting the costs.

Suppose we are not able to book profit even after averaging out four times, i.e., averaging out for four consecutive weeks. In that case, we would revise the profit target to 2.5% after averaging out the fifth time resulting in an investment of ₹5,000. If the investment amount goes up to ₹6,000, profit target would be revised to 2%. After averaging out for seven times, the target would be kept at 1.5%. If profit can't be booked even after that, we would bring down profit target to 1% after averaging out for the eighth time.

Assuming your stock was very weak and you did not get return of even 1% after averaging out eight times, we would maintain the minimum profit target of 0.5% after averaging out the ninth time or any number of times after that.

After averaging out for nine times, your investment in the stock goes up to ₹9,000 and you exit with 0.5% of 9,000, i.e., ₹45 only as profit. This profit is too low, but after adjusting delivery charge and other costs, you would be able to exit, in a way, at 'no profit-no loss'.

In the end, getting 0.5% profit would be quite easy. For example, if your average price were ₹45, even exiting at ₹45.23 would mean a profit target of 0.5%. This would be beneficial in the sense that most of your swing trades would be able to definitely achieve 4.5% to 2.5% profit. The extremely rare situation of 0.5% profit arises only when a stock undergoes a major downturn or market goes through a major and very long bear movement. However, even that has following four advantages:

1. Your core capital of ₹9,000 would get released that you may use for fresh swing trades.
2. Even after adjusting delivery charge of ₹16 and other expenses of ₹18, you are left with ₹11 as net profit. At least you are not exiting with a loss. This gives a great mental satisfaction and you never feel like being stuck with any specific stock.
3. You may earn profit by using this capital for fresh swing trades, else, many traders often remain glued to falling stocks and even their capitals get eroded to half or even one-fourth of original values. They do not get back the price even after 10-15 years. Here, you are getting a chance to exit within two months.
4. You may select a new good stock after exiting from the stock that is falling consecutively for nine weeks! Even if you decide to go for swing trades

in the same stock, just imagine how low that stock that has been falling for nine weeks would have come! Next week, when you invest ₹1,000 in that stock again, you may even get 4.5% return on the same.

As such, there is no need to panic. You would be advised in subsequent chapters how, if you invest in index stocks and out of that also, only Sharegenius leading stocks, your chances of encountering such a situation where you may have to average out for nine weeks or settle with just 0.5% return becomes quite remote, rather almost nil.

□

25

Use Only Index Stocks for Swing Trade

For the swing trade that has been explained in previous tips, you should use only stocks from NIFTY 50, NIFTY Midcap 50, Bank NIFTY and BSE Small Cap, etc.

Why?

As all the well-known fund houses and foreign investors also trade in them, more of volume and fluctuations may be seen in them during the day; hence, you may achieve 4.5% to 2.5% return in most of such trades very easily.

For those readers who have started reading this book from the middle, I should clarify that, in my theory, swing trade refers to trades in cash and carry with holding periods ranging from 1 to 30 days. You should not treat this as intraday trade.

If, unfortunately, despite using an index stock, the stock goes through some fundamental change and the same is removed from the index list, and you continue averaging out once a week at VWAP, the target would keep on falling and settle at 0.5% and you would be able to exit in 9 to 10 weeks in any case. After that, you should not trade in the stock that has been removed from index. You should choose some new index stock in its place.

The *funda* is that using swing trade method with stocks in any of the indexes of NSE or BSE provides better chances of early profit booking.

There is no chance of getting stuck even in the case of a falling stock. That is the scientific feature of this method that you average out only once a week and that also only in strong stocks and even in them, as you average out, you keep bringing your target down. In the end, you become successful in exiting with your basic capital, even earning a small profit.

□

26

Do Not Convert Intraday Into BTST or Swing Trade

One of my friends bought 100 stocks of Yes Bank at the rate of ₹300 in intraday trade. Unfortunately, the stock declined that day and closed at ₹288. He did not have the courage to book a loss of ₹1200 and changed over from intraday to swing trade. He took delivery of the stocks. Later, the stock went down further and came to the level of ₹180 and he changed over to long trade investor. Thus, his trade got converted to long-term investment that is not generating any income. He is just waiting for the stock to move up.

Hence, you need to first of all decide the period for which you are going to trade. And then, you must stick to your decision. For example, if you have bought any stock for a period of one year, you should not keep checking its market price on daily basis and do not think of exiting as and when stock shows sign of decline.

In fact, indiscipline is the main cause of failure in stock market. You should try to toughen your will power. You need practice for the same. You should be careful not to frequently change your decision even in your daily life. As far as possible, be firm on your decision. This would help you strengthen your will power and you would be able to become a successful trader even in the stock market because of your strong will power, else, the stock market never forgives those who keep on changing decision and strategy frequently.

□

27

Greed is a Curse in Stock Market

Greed is a curse in the stock market. When you studied in school in your childhood, you would have certainly read this saying many a time that 'greed is a curse'. But when you trade in stocks, you forget this saying. Most of the people in stock market keep looking for tips that could turn them multimillionaires overnight. Believe me, this is an endless search, as future of any business is always uncertain and it takes years for a business to grow. When you invest in stocks, you need years for a substantial growth. Hence, howsoever perfect a tip may be and whatever be the period of your investment, you should never invest a huge capital in stocks in one go.

Suppose, you feel company 'A' is going to perform very well in future and that stock may get doubled in future and provide up to 100% return. You get greedy and invest one to two lakhs of rupees in the company. Later, if the price does not go up for the next one-two months or, on the contrary, it starts falling, you start getting overwhelmed by stress, frustration and irritation.

Instead, you should do this—start with an investment of only 25% of your capital and keep thinking that if the company really has the guts, let it show a gain of at least

5% and then only I would invest another 25% of my fund. If the stock of the company shows a gain of 10% over its current price, I would invest another 25% and I would invest the rest of 25% also if the price goes up by 15%. This kind of strategy may save you from bad investments.

In this regard, I have one more strategy for increasing-decreasing large investments based on 200 DMA; you may read about the same in detail in my other book—*'How Chandu Earned and Chinki Lost in the Stock Market'*.

□

28

How to Exit a Bad Investment?

If you are reading this book from somewhere in the middle, it's my sincere advice that you first go through the previous tips relating to swing trading fully before reading this tip so that you are able to understand this properly.

One of my colleagues had told me around the year 2006 that it was quite easy to make money in the stock market.

I asked, "How is that?"

At that time, the stock of Dabur India was trading around ₹100. It would rise from ₹100 to the levels of ₹105-103-102 or drop back to ₹98-100. Hence, he thought that if he traded between ₹100 and ₹103 and took return of 3% everyday, he would be able to earn 30% return in a month if he managed to get that return even on ten days in that month.

(I know that this is generally not possible. Sometimes the stock breaks its range and if it drops suddenly to the level of ₹80, the entire money invested for trading at the level of ₹100 would get blocked; but what I am going to tell you may help you make profit even when the range is broken.)

In fact, all small traders enter the stock market initially to make easy money that way only. They even manage to make some money in the beginning. However, later they come to know of some stories about how so-and-so investor had bought some thousands of stocks some 20 years back and did not sell that and now that investor is a multimillionaire.

After listening to such stories in a bull market, they also feel that they are wasting time in trading for small profits. They sometimes get severe jolt also when their stocks go on to double after they book their profits and, thus, their greed turns them from traders to long-term investors. And then, they do not even notice when the market has softly moved to a bear phase. All the profits that they had on paper disappear and, on the contrary, the investments go in red.

Let's assume, a stock is range-bound at ₹90-110. They make some money for a few days by buying the stock at ₹95 and selling at ₹105, but later the stock breaks out and reaches the level of ₹180. They repent having gone for those small trades. They feel the investment would have doubled had they held on to the stocks till that time. Now they are told that it's still time and if they buy even at ₹180, the stock that is a blue chip may go up to ₹1800. They then buy at ₹180 and do not book profits even when the stock goes up to ₹360.

In the meanwhile, bear phase starts. The stock goes up quite slowly but falls very quickly and within 3-4 trading sessions, it comes down to ₹160. This gives a terrible shock to such investors. They do not book that loss of ₹20. They hope to sell the stock when the same rises back to

₹360. But the stock falls down to ₹80 and sticks to a range of 80-88 and keeps moving within that range for the next 2-3 years.

In such a case, their investment made at the level of ₹180 becomes a dead investment that they are just holding for 3-4 years and there is no return on the same. This tip is meant to make such investments alive.

Suppose you had bought 200 stocks at the rate of ₹180 to invest ₹36,000. That stock came down to ₹80 and your investment value got reduced to ₹16,000.

Your stock is fluctuating within the range of ₹80-88, but this movement does not have any value for you.

What should you do when you get stuck in such a situation? Sell the required quantity of stock at any price between ₹80 and ₹88, such that you get ₹1,000. Assuming that you sell 12 stocks at the rate of ₹85, you get ₹1,020. If you adjust ₹20 towards brokerage and delivery charges, you are left with ₹1,000. Just remember that you have 200 stocks. You have booked loss for just 12 stocks out of the same. You are still holding 188 stocks.

Now, you invest this ₹1,000 in stocks of a company selected from NIFTY, ETF or NIFTY 50 as per swing trade tips provided in the previous chapters.

That means, you select such a stock out of 50 stocks in NIFTY 50 that is priced below ₹1,000.

Place a limit order at previous day's VWAP for the quantity of stock that can be bought for ₹1,000. Next week, repeat the same process. Whenever you get a profit of 4.5% to 0.5% on your average holding, book your profit and exit. (We have already discussed in detail over profit targets from 4.5% to 1% in the previous tips.)

The above process would provide following benefits to you:

1. You do not need to book loss in all stocks at a time. You have to book loss in only one stock at a time—that also limited to the quantity that would fetch you an amount of ₹1,000. This would provide you a chance to book profits just in case the stock gets a bounce back.
2. Your dead investment may start generating profit somewhere between 4.5% and 0.5% that would help you recover your losses.
3. Gradually, your investment in moribund stocks would shift to dividend-paying stocks of NIFTY 50.
4. If you plan to use swing trade only for your trading in stocks in future, you may use those moribund stocks lying in your portfolio for a long time instead of investing fresh capital.

□

29

Don't Bother About Bonus

In a stock market, ignorance about bonus is the reason for maximum loss to the investors. In fact, all such investors have heard many stories relating to well-known IT companies, for example, somebody was holding 100 stocks of so-and-so company in 1991 and the company kept on paying bonus regularly to the extent that 100 stocks increased to 200 stocks, 200 went up to 400, 400 went up to 800 and 800 also went up to 1,600 stocks. The stock holding has gone up to 50,000 today, after many such bonuses and divisions of face value of the stock. The stock price is ₹500 today and, thus, the valuation of his holding has gone up to ₹2.5 crores.

A person gets swayed by greed after listening to such stories. Whenever any company declares bonus, he buys and holds its stocks. Taking advantage of this kind of mentality of common investors, even companies with weak fundamentals declare bonus, resulting in a jump in its stock price, and company promoters exploit that opportunity and exit.

A perfect example for the same is the stock of Unitech that jumped from ₹156.65 to the highest level of ₹14,798.55 in 2006 after declaration of 12 bonus stocks on one existing stock. Unitech again declared 1:1 bonus share in the year 2007 and the stock got a fresh jump. However, the stock later went on a decline and slowly came down to the level of ₹1.05 in the year 2019.

In fact, in the case of large IT companies, that growth in valuation of 100 stocks to crores was a result of increase in the income of those companies and not because of issue of bonus.

A bonus issue results in reduction in the price of that stock in the same proportion. Had these famous IT companies like Wipro and Infosys not issued any bonus, their single stock would have been priced in crores today and it would have been quite difficult for normal investors to buy the same. That's the reason periodical issue of bonus is necessary to keep market price of stocks in the range of investors.

As the income and prospects of a company go up, its market price also increases in proportion of its income and profits. In the situation, issue of bonus stocks reduces income per stock and, hence, market price of the stock also goes down proportionately.

Hence, make sure you do not invest in stocks based on the declaration of bonus issues. Invest in stocks based on the income and profits of the company.

□

30

Averaging Out is not Bad Every Time

You have read in Tip No. 10 that you should not average out a falling position.

This is true for an intraday position, but averaging out is not bad in all situations. For example, in the case of a mutual fund, you use SIP (Systematic Investment Plan) to buy units for a specific amount every month; that is in a way averaging out the units only.

Similarly, the process of swing trade that has been explained in previous tips is also based on a disciplined way of averaging out index stocks from NIFTY, etc., to earn returns between 4.5% and 0.5% on average costs.

This process is so effective that you would become its fan once you use the same, as you buy stocks once in a week or once in a month for a definite amount and you keep on revising your profit target down with every average out action; this ensures that you do get an average return of around 2.5% and also an opportunity to exit safely for every position. You have to just keep accumulating good dividend-paying index stocks bit-by-bit averaging out every week or every month at previous day's VWAP. This has been explained in detail in previous tips.

□

31

Either Become a Genuine Long Term Investor or Use Swing Trading

Those who have read my previous book 'The Winning Theory in the Stock Market' or have gone through my research term on my blog would be aware of the fact that I give preference to fundamental ratios like base price, net sale per stock, etc., for identifying a value stock before buying the same. However, the stock market fall during the year 2018 made me go for some contemplation.

In fact, when I was trading alone, had I bought stocks of Eicher Motors in the year 2007 at the rate of ₹599 based on these facts, I would not have gone through any anxiety/grief/anger/frustration even when the same crashed to ₹135 during the year 2008. I would not have also felt stuck in a position as I had a long-term viewpoint and I used to invest a maximum of 10% of my monthly income in a single stock. That time, my monthly salary was ₹15,000 and, accordingly, my investment would have been limited to ₹1,500 and I would have hardly got 3 stocks. Hence, I would not have got worried or felt stressed on losing that amount of ₹1,500 and even the stock like Eicher Motors getting delisted. However, ever since I have started recommending stocks from a public platform after getting registered as a Research Analyst, I have come to know that all my 71,000 followers are not the same. They get greedy and invest in lakhs in single lots and if the stock falls from ₹599 to a level of ₹135, they start calling me names in their comments.

It may be appropriate to mention here that Eicher Motors that had declined from ₹599 to ₹135 during the year 2008 had reached a level of ₹32,200 in the year 2018; but my followers would not wait for ten years. I had to devise this process of swing trade for such followers.

You have already read about swing trade in previous chapters.

Overall, the main point of this tip is that you have two choices for investment. One, you invest small amounts (as per my rules, 10% of your monthly income) in your favourite stocks and hold the same peacefully for 5-10-15 years. Then, even if such an investment loses its value and comes below its original cost, you should not worry and patiently wait for a turnaround in performance of the company, as happened in the context of Eicher Motors. You should not get worried if the company keeps declining and even gets delisted (as happened with my investment in Tantia Construction) during that wait. You have invested in 100 companies and even if 2-3 companies fail or get closed, you are still left with 97 working companies.

Two, you may go for swing trade, as, in a swing trade, you never feel like being stuck and even if you have to exit with a profit of 0.5% on average price after going through multiple averaging outs, you would get back your capital and you may use the same capital next week for fresh investment in the same stock at a lower price with profit target of 4.5%.

□

32

Why Should You Invest in Index Stocks?

There is a saying in the stock market—if you can't beat the index, go with the index.

Suppose, you started investing in stock market when NIFTY was at the level of 8,000. NIFTY is at 10,800 today. That means, NIFTY has gone up by 30% during the period of your investment.

If you made a profit of over 30% during the period of your investment, you may be treated as a good and proficient investor (most of the small investors, on the contrary, lose value of their portfolio by 30%).

That is the reason that even mutual fund managers treat some index as their benchmarks.

ETFs have been designed on the same principle. For example, NIFTY BeES or NIFTY ETFs invest in all the stocks of NIFTY Index in the proportion same as their share in NIFTY. Hence, their market prices hover around 1/10th or 1/100th (as per the price decided by ETF for its units) of NIFTY and small investors may continue moving with index by investing in them through systematic investment plan (SIP), just like a mutual fund.

□

33

Choose NIFTY Stocks for Trading as well as Swing Trading

All the 50 stocks of NIFTY 50 are also traded in Futures and Options segment of the stock market. Domestic mutual funds and foreign institutional investors (FIIs) also trade in the same stocks. Almost 80% to 90% of trades in the market are done in those very stocks and, hence, they enjoy sufficient liquidity while they also go through good enough fluctuations. Hence, in my opinion, stocks from NIFTY 50 should be selected for intraday trading or swing trading (even among them, which ones should be chosen—this would be explained later).

Secondly, stocks included in indexes like NIFTY, SENSEX, etc., are selected by exchange committees after testing them on the criteria of volume, profits, dividend liability, etc.

Stocks included in indexes are appraised periodically and such stocks that do not meet the criteria of market cap, volume, dividend, etc., are removed and replaced by new stocks.

Accordingly, you may use the method explained in subsequent chapters to exit from stocks being removed from NIFTY without booking any loss and invest in fresh stocks getting included there. This will be discussed in detail in the next tip.

□

34

Review Swing Trade Portfolio Just Like Index

As has been explained in the previous tip, there are some standards for selection of stocks for indexes, like NIFTY, SENSEX, etc. These standards are set by well-known experts in economics to ensure that only best companies are included in such indexes.

But, when a company is not able to meet those standards because of its poor performance, such a company is removed from index after the process of periodical assessment of index companies and in its place, a new company that meets those standards is included in the index.

Hence, if you are engaged in swing trades after selecting stocks from NIFTY/SENSEX following the process explained in previous tips and any of your selected stocks is removed from index, you should also stop trading in that stock after booking profit in the same and pick a fresh stock from NIFTY/SENSEX in its place for inclusion in your swing trade portfolio.

That means if the stock that has been removed from index starts declining, you should still continue to average out the same every week based on previous day's VWAP and eventually, after you exit without loss whenever you get 0.5% profit on your average price, you may pick a new stock from index in place of that removed stock.

□

35

How to Pick Stocks for Trading?

As has been explained to you up already, I would give preference to BTST (buy today, sell tomorrow) over intraday and to swing trade (where a stock is averaged out every week until a return between 4.5% and 0.5% over average price is achieved) over BTST.

I would even go to the extent of giving you a noble advice as your elder brother that you stick to swing trade only in NIFTY/SENSEX stocks, as the same is not only safe but also provides you the means to turn your investment of ₹10,000 into ₹1.24 crores in 30 years even if you are able to generate average return of only 2% every month. Much has been discussed in this regard in previous chapters.

For swing trade, you need to pick stocks from NIFTY 50—this has already been explained to you. However, you should look into 52-week highs even for those stocks. You should pick the stocks that are trading near (maximum 15% below) their 52-week highs, i.e., the highest level during the year.

Why?

Because stock market runs on the instincts of greed and fear. Hence, when a stock keeps declining and ultimately reaches the lowest level of the year, stop-loss of investors start getting triggered and even those investors start selling that stock, resulting in further decline.

Another theory is that stock market knows everything. In this age of information technology, if a company is expecting a decline in their forthcoming performance, this fact gets leaked through various internal sources and finds its way to the market even before the news comes out in the open. In the language of stock market, this is called 'rumour'. You may call it a rumour, but even such rumours are not wrong in 80% of the cases, and though it may take a time of six months to a year, these rumours are proven right quite often. Hence, if a stock comes to its 52-week low without any specific reason, it is generally observed that the stock keeps on declining further and making new lows every 10 to 15 days. Exactly the same thing happens in the case of a stock trading at its highest level or near its 52-week high. Such a stock keeps on making new highs at a fast pace. Trading in such stocks provides you several opportunities to book small profits (4.5% to 0.5%) at frequent intervals.

Thus, the *funda* is that selecting those very 10-15 stocks out of NIFTY/SENSEX stocks that are trading at their highest levels of the year or trading within a range of 0% to 15% of their highest levels may provide profits at a faster pace.

Here, it may also be relevant to mention this maxim of the stock market—'If you buy cheap stocks, you would sell cheap; if you buy premium stocks, you would sell at premium.'

You may be wondering, "While trading near high, what if I get stuck in a high position? I mean, what if I have to face 'misfortune in the very first adventure', i.e., the stock may be at its peak right at the time I bought the same and after that, the stock just keeps on falling?" This will be answered in subsequent tips.

□

36

A Stock Never Declines Endlessly

As you have seen in the previous tip, stock of a company starts falling even six months to one year before actual decline in the performance of that company, as the rumours leaked by internal sources of the company keep finding their way to the market.

However, when the stock starts falling after the rumour is out, some greedy investors start buying the same thinking that they should not lose the chance of acquiring such a costly bluechip stock at such a cheap rate. On the other side, even some long-term fundamental investors slowly start investing in the same, as in the case of fundamentally strong stock, even if its performance declines for a year or two, its pace of recovery is also quite fast when its performance picks up.

Hence, such purchases made by small investors because of their tendency to buy stocks that have crashed by half (though this tendency is not correct; you have already read in my previous book '*How to Make Profit in Share Market*' that the stock having 52-week high/52-week low over 2 should not be bought for long-term investment) or made by long-term fundamental investors as they start investing in such stocks in instalments, enable the stock to start gaining slowly even after the rumour is out. People think that the rumour has been proven wrong and as the stock has started appreciating, they should buy the same. This further gives a temporary jump to the stock price. But, after that, the stock falls even more than what it had gained.

To understand this practically, let us take the examples of Yes Bank and IOC. Both the stocks are included in NIFTY and both had crashed badly from their year highs during 2018.

Let's have a look at their charts below.

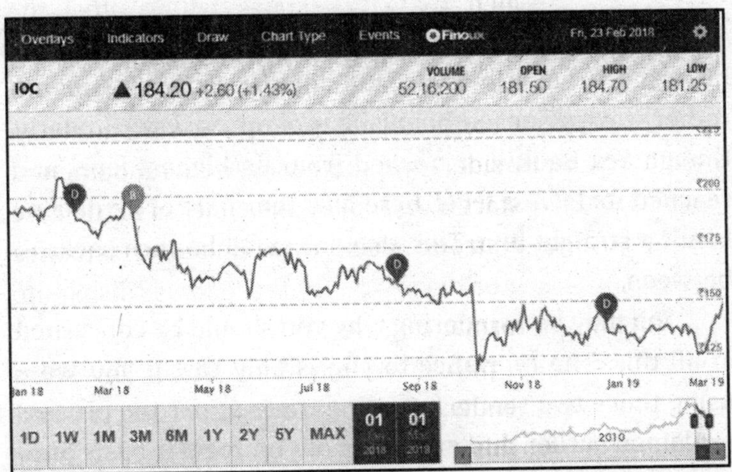

(IOC—January 2018 to March 2019)

(Yes Bank—January 2018 to March 2019)

You can see that though IOC has crashed from its highest level to a low level, its fall has not been smooth; rather it experienced bounce backs on its way. Similarly, though Yes Bank has crashed from its highest level and reached its lowest level, here also the chart of its decline is not a straight line. This also has small bounce backs in between.

You may be wondering why you should be concerned of all this. The relevance to you is only that if you were using those two stocks for swing trade as per the process explained earlier, and averaging out on regular basis once in a week at previous day's VWAP, then, even if you had bought them at their highest levels of the year, you could easily exit after booking 2%-3% profit over your average prices by taking advantage of these small bounce backs. After your exit, you could have reviewed and found that the stocks were not in the range of 15% from their 52-week highs anymore and, hence, would have selected from NIFTY some other stocks trading near their 52-week high.

I have a YouTube video also on this subject, where I have explained how IOC stock crashed almost 65% in a year and, with the help of swing trade, you could have booked profit 8 times even during that 65% crash.

□

37

Advantages of Trading in the Dividend-Paying Stocks

You would have understood by now that, for trading, I advise choosing such large cap stocks from NIFTY 50 or SENSEX 30 that are trading near their 52-week highs. But, why is it like that? You would have certainly got this question in your mind—'why shouldn't I trade in such small cap or mid cap stocks, suggested by you or any other analyst, that I feel may give a return of 200%-300% in one or two years?'

Well, the answer is that you must, first of all, have the capacity to hold fundamental stocks; this is normally not found in small investors as explained by me in previous tips with an example of Eicher Motors.

Secondly, you must have heard the story of one Sethji; if not, let me tell you the same. There was a Sethji who was a typical miser. He would usually eat stale rotis with salt and chilli only and no vegetables, just to save money on vegetables. But, in order to satiate his desire for vegetables and other delicacies, he would keep his eyes closed for 10 minutes after his meal and go into meditation imagining that he was enjoying a sumptuous meal with daal and curry.

Such meditations used to satisfy his desires. Once, when he was in a state of similar meditation, he felt the curry to be too spicy and he started making a sound like 'Cee-Cee'.

When a passer-by heard that sound, he asked him, "Sethji, what happened?" Sethji told him the full story how he was eating food in his imagination and how he felt his mouth to be burning because of very spicy curry, resulting in that sound. That person said, "You fool Seth, if you have to enjoy food in your imagination only, why do you eat only daal-curry? Eat sweets, dry fruits, kaju-katli and fresh fruits, and if you have to eat daal-curry only in your imagination, you should eat the same cooked by a good chef with perfect spices that would not burn your mouth."

In this tip, I am trying to give a message something similar to the above story—if you have to make profits between 4.5% and 0.5% only, why should you invest in risky stocks?

Any fundamental stock that has the potential to give multiple returns in future is equally risky too. It is natural also, as such a stock would be recommended only when the same can be included in the category of 'value buy'. When the market price of a stock is lower than its 'Net Sale Per Share' and its book value, the stock is recommended by any research analyst, treating the same as a 'value stock'.

However, there is also a risk here. If some news relating to any problem that a company is going to face in future is leaked in the market before the same is known to the public in general, the market price of that stock may come down to the extent that we may buy the same assuming it to be a value buy.

Such leaked news about company problems is called 'rumour'. The same thing happened with the stocks of Kingfisher, Tantia Construction, Pratibha Industries, Satyam Computers and DHFL, etc., when their market prices went below their 'Net Sale Per Share' figures and their book values and they were treated as fundamental value buys. But later, as the news about these companies started coming out in the open, the stocks crashed by 60% to 90%.

Hence, if you want to earn 200%-500% return with long-term holding, then, as you have read in my book 'अब्दुल स्टॉक मार्केट में ज़ीरो से हीरो कैसे बना', you may invest up to a maximum of 10% of your monthly income in such stocks coming in the category of fundamental value buy and expect multiple returns by holding them for 2-3 years. But, if you are planning to use swing trade to earn 4.5% to 0.5% returns within a period of one day to one month, why should you take risk for the same? Why not to invest only in such stocks of NIFTY/SENSEX that are trading near their year-highs? Such stocks are normally less risky. They also have good volumes and bounce backs for 4.5% to 0.5% profit can be found in a short time, and when they are held, they also bring bonus and dividends.

□

38

Income Tax Harvesting to Save Capital Gains

In this tip, I will tell you how to go about income tax farming or tax harvesting in stock market.

Yes, income tax farming in stock market is a well-known process that is called 'income tax harvesting' in USA. In American politics, Mr. Trump was once accused of not paying full income tax on his income from the stock market. It was clarified at that time that he had not done anything illegal. What he had done is called tax harvesting or income tax farming that is totally legal and that facilitates avoidance of tax on capital gains made in a stock market. You would learn the same tax harvesting in this tip.

In fact, this has a very simple arithmetic. For the entire year, you keep on making small investments in good dividend paying stocks as explained in previous tips. Book profits in the stocks that gain as per your targets. Hold on to the rest of the stocks and enjoy dividends.

During the last few days of March, you may go for income tax harvesting for the stocks that you are holding.

Actually, this is very simple. During the last few days of March, sell all those stocks in your portfolio that are in red and book losses on paper; but, at the same time, same day, buy the same stocks back in the same quantity at the same moment immediately after selling.

What do you get out of this?

This will not have any impact on the quantity of stocks, as we are buying the same quantity of stocks on the same day, same time as that of the stocks sold for booking loss.

We would have to only pay brokerage that is generally quite low these days with discount brokers. Even to save that brokerage, you may keep some small difference between your sale and purchase prices; but the loss that we have booked may be adjusted against the profits booked during the entire year, thereby reducing the resultant short-term capital gains.

How?

Suppose, you have made a total profit of ₹60,000 till 20 March, 2019 by booking profits in various stocks during the current year. As per income tax regulations, you would have to pay short term capital gains tax amounting to ₹9,000 being 15% of the total gains.

Let's assume the stocks that we are still holding as on 20 March are showing a loss of ₹45,000. We would sell these stocks to book losses and buy back the same quantity of the stocks. After adjusting this loss of ₹45,000 against profit of ₹60,000, we would be left with net profit for the year as ₹15,000 only. We would have to pay short-term capital gains tax on this amount only, i.e., ₹2,250 at the rate of 15%. Thus, tax liability is reduced from ₹9,000 to ₹2,250 only and this is what is called income tax harvesting.

Even if you have to pay ₹750 towards brokerage in the above process, you are still saving a net amount of ₹6,000 on capital gains tax.

Here, some of the readers may raise a doubt that selling and buying stocks on the same day may be treated as intraday, i.e., speculation income and how would we adjust the amount of that loss against short-term capital loss? The answer to the same is this. If you are already holding the stock and you select cash and carry option while placing the order, that kind of sale of stock is not treated as intraday trading. You have just booked loss in your stocks already held with you.

Similarly, fresh stock is also bought through a fresh order with cash and carry option paying full amount and delivery of the same is also taken; hence, this is a new trade. Whenever we sell this stock, tax on the profit would be decided based on the period of holding. Thus, selling the stock already under holding through a cash and carry order and taking full payment and also taking delivery of the same would not be treated as intraday trade.

□

39

Use 4-Stroke Method for Options Trading

I have practically tried a number of methods for options trading. Complete details of the same, though, would be provided in my forthcoming book on options trading, but I have found 4-stroke method as the best out of all of them.

You may achieve success in 80%-90% of your trades in options using this 4-stroke method.

As has already been explained earlier, there is no 100% perfect system for trading in the stock market. However, you may still be a winning trader if the rate of success of your system is 80%-90%.

Using this method, you may take positions in options in NIFTY and Bank NIFTY. Though, if you want, you may use this very method to take positions in call/put options in a particular stock instead of an index.

However, it is advisable to take options positions in NIFTY or Bank NIFTY instead of any specific stock, as there is no issue of liquidity in their case. When you take a position in a specific stock, you may encounter problems due to low liquidity despite this method being correct.

Let me now explain this 4-stroke method.

Let's assume, on a particular day, the close price

of NIFTY Future was ₹1,873.30 after the closure of the market.

In this method, we would check the closing price of Future for the day instead of the closing price of NIFTY.

Now, you have to prepare in advance for trading on the next day based on this closing price. You have to note down on paper the nearest 'in-the-money call and in-the-money put' of this closing price for the nearest expiry month (if you are trying this method in Bank NIFTY, you have to choose call/put of the nearest weekly expiry). For example, if closing price of futures is ₹10,873.30, the nearest in-the-money call for the same would be ₹10,850 and nearest in-the-money put has to be taken as ₹10,900.

Now, you have to note down high and low of above call and put for that day's trading (you may watch my YouTube tutorial to learn how to view historical price data for call/put in options).

Let's assume the highest and lowest premiums of the day for the call of ₹10,850 were ₹163.30 and ₹86.45, respectively; you should note down both the figures.

Now, note down the highest and lowest premiums for put of ₹10,900. Suppose they are ₹175.35 and ₹96.40, respectively. Thus, you have four figures with you now (that's why I have named this method as '4-stroke method').

You are now ready with a chart for the next day. This may look like this:

Options	Strike Price	Highest Level	Lowest Level
Call	10,850	163.30	86.45
Put	10,900	175.35	96.40

Next day, keep a watch on the premium on the call of ₹10,850, after opening of the market. If the premium opens above previous day's highest level of ₹163.30 or breaks out above the same, you should buy the call of ₹10,850 immediately at that very moment and exit once you get a profit of ₹10 on the same, i.e., if you buy at ₹165.80, you should book profit at ₹175.80. I have taken ₹165.80 as example above, instead of previous day's high figure of ₹163.30, because call normally rises quite fast in the case of such a break out and by the time you take a position, the same would have gone up at least to some extent.

If the next day, this call of ₹10,850 opens below previous day's low of ₹86.45 or goes below the same, you should short this call of ₹10,850. It is safest to keep the profit target as ₹10 only in this, i.e., if you have taken short position at ₹85.50, you should book profit once the same falls to ₹75.50. The size of one lot of NIFTY is 75; thus, booking a profit of ₹10 means total profit of ₹750.

In this 4-stroke method, you get a profit of ₹10 within just 5 to 10 minutes when there is a breakout from previous day's high or low.

Similarly, if the put of ₹10,900 breaks out above previous day's high of ₹175.35 or opens above that high, you should take a buy position in the same and exit after booking profit of ₹10.

If the put of ₹10,900 falls below previous day's low of ₹96.40 or opens below that low, you should go for a short position in the same and exit after booking profit of ₹10.

In the case of Bank NIFTY, the lot size is just 20. You may keep your profit target between ₹15 and ₹20, as you may have to pay brokerage also.

In the same way, you may also use this 4-stroke method to buy call/put for any specific stock. If you have to fix your profit target in the premium by percentage, you may fix the same around 5% of the premium. For example, if previous day's highest level for your specific call was ₹405.60 and you buy the same when it breaks out at ₹410, your target should be fixed at 5% of ₹410, i.e., around 20 rupees. It is not advisable to be too greedy here as call/put fall also with the same speed as that with which they rise.

Now the question arises—what should be the level of stop-loss in this method?

Time-based stop-loss is the best in this method, i.e., you should use a 5-minute stop-loss, as, if your breakout is real, a profit of 5% or 10-15 rupees is achieved within those 5 minutes. If you do not achieve your profit target within those 5 minutes, you should gather courage and close your position with whatever profit or loss you are making.

I am advising time-based stop-loss because call/put normally go up and down with great speed and wide fluctuations and a close stop-loss would have a high probability of getting hit quickly.

When your target itself is just 5%, stop-loss, as per rules, would be half of the same, i.e., 2.5% only. As the same is too low, there is a chance of your stop-loss getting hit first and your target getting achieved after that. Hence, use of 5-minute stop-loss is preferable.

Before using this method in practice, you should do some theoretical exercise. You would get a sense of the level of stop-loss to be used.

□

40

Options Trading is Better than Intraday

Trading in options was launched in NSE in the year 2001. That time, options did not have satisfactory volumes, but today, most of the day traders have migrated from intraday trading to options trading. If you take call-put position in options, your risks are limited, i.e., the maximum that you may lose is the premium of that call or put.

If you are using intraday trading in options, you get more leverage at lower prices. By the way, it is not the subject matter of this book to provide full information on options trading, as the same is not possible in this small book. In case you are not conversant with options trading, you may go through some book on this subject by another writer or wait for my forthcoming options-special book.

The purpose of this tip is only to tell you that if you want to trade in a specific stock, you should go for options trading instead of intraday trading.

However, options trading is not meant for small investors. You should take up this only if you have a large capital. As an example, if Ramesh buys ₹3,500 stocks of

Hindalco @ ₹200 in intraday, he has to pay a minimum margin of ₹1,50,000 on his trade value of ₹7,00,000, whereas Hitesh can buy a call option of ₹200 of Hindalco for ₹9 only, and as its lot size is 3,500, he has to pay ₹31,500 only as options premium.

If Hitesh is following the 4-stroke method explained earlier for his trade, he would buy the call of ₹200 when the same goes above the previous day's high, and if he is able to buy at ₹9 and sell the same at ₹10, he may earn ₹3,500 in this trade. But, do remember, options trading is also risky just like intraday trading. Hence, you have been advised in the previous tip that a new trader should start practice with only a single lot of Bank NIFTY. Lot size of Bank NIFTY is 20 only and, hence, if you trade in the same in intraday for 15-20 rupees as per the previous tip, not only you would not have any risk of a big loss, but you also would get a practice in options trading.

Here, let me repeat that, in my opinion, swing trade is the best method. This would keep satisfying your pursuits of both investment and trading and if you follow the process explained earlier, your risk would be virtually nil.

The second best method is options trading in Bank NIFTY and NIFTY using 4-stroke process.

Intraday trading in stocks comes at the third position.

You would be advised about the maximum holding period for options in the next tip.

□

41

Don't Trade Based on Market News and Advices from the So-called Experts

Stock markets never run based on news. You don't have to listen to fake advices from the so-called experts. They would say—"American President has tweeted on trade war; market is not going to go up now." Another time, they would say—"Now this bear phase is going to be long." Still another time, they may say—"We had already informed you in the morning that market was going to go up today." And it almost crossed the limits when some of the experts opined, "Moon was red during lunar eclipse; this is called 'blood moon'. This happens once in many years and this red colour is indicating that stock market is going to fall."

If you keep on looking for others' advices, you are definitely going to lose. Don't follow even my advice. You should believe in your system; you should believe in yourself. You have to keep on repeating only this mantra—'There is no good or bad stock in the market. There is no good or bad market. There are only gaining and losing stocks in the market. Market either goes up or declines. This is the only rule in the market. All other things are useless.'

Remember, ups and downs in the stock market have always been there and would always be there. In this reference, I am just recollecting the following words of a saint:

ख़ून पसीना बहाता जा, तान के चादर सोता जा।
यह नाव तो हिलती जाएगी, तू हँसता जा या रोता जा।।

Thus, the boat of the market does swing while moving ahead and it does not matter if you blame it on a tweet from Trump or on a surgical strike or on a 'blood moon'. Ups and downs are the basic principles of the market. How would you trade in the absence of ups and downs? You have to just concentrate on using those ups and downs for your benefit instead of throwing your hard-earned capital into the market just on the basis of news and without any theory.

In the end, I put my pen to rest saying that my formulas on swing trade, that have been explained in this book, are the most risk free and have the potential to provide the best returns. There is an Appendix at the end of this book showing how an amount of ₹10,000 grows to ₹1.24 crores after 360 trades if you manage to earn even 2% return on your trades. Please don't forget to write a 5-star review for my book after going through that table, as your 5-star review would infuse me with energy and I would be able to work on my forthcoming book on options with more vigour.

With best compliments,

Yours sincerely,
Mahesh Chander Kaushik

□

Appendix A—In Reference To Tip No. 4

Month	Initial Investment	2% Profit for the Whole Month	Balance at the End of the Month
1	10,000.00	200.00	10,200.00
2	10,200.00	204.00	10,404.00
3	10,404.00	208.08	10,612.08
4	10,612.08	212.24	10,824.32
5	10,824.32	216.49	11,040.81
6	11,040.81	220.82	11,261.63
7	11,261.63	225.23	11,486.86
8	11,486.86	229.74	11,716.59
9	11,716.59	234.33	11,950.92
10	11,950.92	239.02	12,189.94
11	12,189.94	243.80	12,433.74
12	12,433.74	248.67	12,682.42
13	12,682.42	253.65	12,936.07
14	12,936.07	258.72	13,194.79
15	13,194.79	263.90	13,458.69
16	13,458.69	269.17	13,727.86
17	13,727.86	274.56	14,002.42
18	14,002.42	280.05	14,282.47

Month	Initial Investment	2% Profit for the Whole Month	Balance at the End of the Month
19	14,282.47	285.65	14,568.12
20	14,568.12	291.36	14,859.48
21	14,859.48	297.18	15,156.66
22	15,156.66	303.14	15,459.80
23	15,459.80	309.19	15,768.99
24	15,768.99	315.38	16,084.37
25	16,084.37	321.69	16,406.06
26	16,406.06	328.12	16,734.18
27	16,734.18	334.68	17,068.86
28	17,068.86	341.38	17,410.24
29	17,410.24	348.21	17,758.45
30	17,758.45	355.17	18,113.62
31	18,113.62	362.27	18,475.89
32	18,475.89	369.52	18,845.41
33	18,845.41	376.90	19,222.31
34	19,222.31	384.45	19,606.76
35	19,606.76	392.14	19,998.90
36	19,998.90	399.97	20,398.87
37	20,398.87	407.98	20,806.85

Month	Initial Investment	2% Profit for the Whole Month	Balance at the End of the Month
38	20,806.85	416.14	21,222.99
39	21,222.99	424.46	21,647.45
40	21,647.45	432.95	22,080.40
41	22,080.40	441.60	22,522.00
42	22,522.00	450.44	22,972.44
43	22,972.44	459.45	23,431.89
44	23,431.89	468.64	23,900.53
45	23,900.53	478.01	24,378.54
46	24,378.54	487.57	24,866.11
47	24,866.11	497.33	25,363.44
48	25,363.44	507.26	25,870.70
49	25,870.70	517.42	26,388.12
50	26,388.12	527.76	26,915.88
51	26,915.88	538.32	27,454.20
52	27,454.20	549.08	28,003.28
53	28,003.28	560.07	28,563.35
54	28,563.35	571.26	29,134.61
55	29,134.61	582.70	29,717.31
56	29,717.31	594.34	30,311.65

Month	Initial Investment	2% Profit for the Whole Month	Balance at the End of the Month
57	30,311.65	606.24	30,917.89
58	30,917.89	618.35	31,536.24
59	31,536.24	630.73	32,166.97
60	32,166.97	643.34	32,810.31
61	32,810.31	656.20	33,466.51
62	33,466.51	669.33	34,135.84
63	34,135.84	682.72	34,818.56
64	34,818.56	696.37	35,514.93
65	35,514.93	710.30	36,225.23
66	36,225.23	724.51	36,949.74
67	36,949.74	738.99	37,688.73
68	37,688.73	753.78	38,442.51
69	38,442.51	768.85	39,211.36
70	39,211.36	784.22	39,995.58
71	39,995.58	799.91	40,795.49
72	40,795.49	815.91	41,611.40
73	41,611.40	832.23	42,443.63
74	42,443.63	848.87	43,292.50
75	43,292.50	865.85	44,158.35

Month	Initial Investment	2% Profit for the Whole Month	Balance at the End of the Month
76	44,158.35	883.17	45,041.52
77	45,041.52	900.83	45,942.35
78	45,942.35	918.85	46,861.20
79	46,861.20	937.22	47,798.42
80	47,798.42	955.97	48,754.39
81	48,754.39	975.09	49,729.48
82	49,729.48	994.59	50,724.07
83	50,724.07	1,014.48	51,738.55
84	51,738.55	1,034.77	52,773.32
85	52,773.32	1,055.47	53,828.79
86	53,828.79	1,076.57	54,905.36
87	54,905.36	1,098.11	56,003.47
88	56,003.47	1,120.07	57,123.54
89	57,123.54	1,142.47	58,266.01
90	58,266.01	1,165.32	59,431.33
91	59,431.33	1,188.63	60,619.96
92	60,619.96	1,212.40	61,832.36
93	61,832.36	1,236.64	63,069.00
94	63,069.00	1,261.38	64,330.38

Month	Initial Investment	2% Profit for the Whole Month	Balance at the End of the Month
95	64,330.38	1,286.61	65,616.99
96	65,616.99	1,312.34	66,929.33
97	66,929.33	1,338.59	68,267.92
98	68,267.92	1,365.36	69,633.28
99	69,633.28	1,392.66	71,025.94
100	71,025.94	1,420.52	72,446.46
101	72,446.46	1,448.93	73,895.39
102	73,895.39	1,477.91	75,373.30
103	75,373.30	1,507.46	76,880.76
104	76,880.76	1,537.62	78,418.38
105	78,418.38	1,568.37	79,986.75
106	79,986.75	1,599.73	81,586.48
107	81,586.48	1,631.73	83,218.21
108	83,218.21	1,664.37	84,882.58
109	84,882.58	1,697.65	86,580.23
110	86,580.23	1,731.60	88,311.83
111	88,311.83	1,766.24	90,078.07
112	90,078.07	1,801.56	91,879.63
113	91,879.63	1,837.59	93,717.22

Month	Initial Investment	2% Profit for the Whole Month	Balance at the End of the Month
114	93,717.22	1,874.35	95,591.57
115	95,591.57	1,911.83	97,503.40
116	97,503.40	1,950.07	99,453.47
117	99,453.47	1,989.07	1,01,442.54
118	1,01,442.54	2,028.85	1,03,471.39
119	1,03,471.39	2,069.42	1,05,540.81
120	1,05,540.81	2,110.82	1,07,651.63
121	1,07,651.63	2,153.03	1,09,804.66
122	1,09,804.66	2,196.09	1,12,000.76
123	1,12,000.76	2,240.02	1,14,240.77
124	1,14,240.77	2,284.82	1,16,525.59
125	1,16,525.59	2,330.51	1,18,856.10
126	1,18,856.10	2,377.12	1,21,233.22
127	1,21,233.22	2,424.66	1,23,657.88
128	1,23,657.88	2,473.16	1,26,131.04
129	1,26,131.04	2,522.62	1,28,653.66
130	1,28,653.66	2,573.08	1,31,226.74
131	1,31,226.74	2,624.53	1,33,851.27
132	1,33,851.27	2,677.03	1,36,528.30

Month	Initial Investment	2% Profit for the Whole Month	Balance at the End of the Month
133	1,36,528.30	2,730.56	1,39,258.86
134	1,39,258.86	2,785.18	1,42,044.04
135	1,42,044.04	2,840.88	1,44,884.92
136	1,44,884.92	2,897.70	1,47,782.62
137	1,47,782.62	2,955.65	1,50,738.27
138	1,50,738.27	3,014.77	1,53,753.04
139	1,53,753.04	3,075.06	1,56,828.10
140	1,56,828.10	3,136.56	1,59,964.66
141	1,59,964.66	3,199.29	1,63,163.95
142	1,63,163.95	3,263.28	1,66,427.23
143	1,66,427.23	3,328.55	1,69,755.78
144	1,69,755.78	3,395.11	1,73,150.89
145	1,73,150.89	3,463.02	1,76,613.91
146	1,76,613.91	3,532.28	1,80,146.19
147	1,80,146.19	3,602.92	1,83,749.11
148	1,83,749.11	3,674.98	1,87,424.09
149	1,87,424.09	3,748.49	1,91,172.58
150	1,91,172.58	3,823.45	1,94,996.03
151	1,94,996.03	3,899.92	1,98,895.95

Month	Initial Investment	2% Profit for the Whole Month	Balance at the End of the Month
152	1,98,895.95	3,977.92	2,02,873.87
153	2,02,873.87	4,057.47	2,06,931.34
154	2,06,931.34	4,138.63	2,11,069.97
155	2,11,069.97	4,221.40	2,15,291.37
156	2,15,291.37	4,305.83	2,19,597.20
157	2,19,597.20	4,391.94	2,23,989.14
158	2,23,989.14	4,479.79	2,28,468.93
159	2,28,468.93	4,569.37	2,33,038.30
160	2,33,038.30	4,660.77	2,37,699.07
161	2,37,699.07	4,753.98	2,42,453.05
162	2,42,453.05	4,849.06	2,47,302.11
163	2,47,302.11	4,946.04	2,52,248.15
164	2,52,248.15	5,044.97	2,57,293.12
165	2,57,293.12	5,145.86	2,62,438.98
166	2,62,438.98	5,248.78	2,67,687.76
167	2,67,687.76	5,353.75	2,73,041.51
168	2,73,041.51	5,460.83	2,78,502.34
169	2,78,502.34	5,570.05	2,84,072.39
170	2,84,072.39	5,681.45	2,89,753.84

Month	Initial Investment	2% Profit for the Whole Month	Balance at the End of the Month
171	2,89,753.84	5,795.08	2,95,548.92
172	2,95,548.92	5,910.97	3,01,459.89
173	3,01,459.89	6,029.20	3,07,489.09
174	3,07,489.09	6,149.78	3,13,638.87
175	3,13,638.87	6,272.78	3,19,911.65
176	3,19,911.65	6,398.23	3,26,309.88
177	3,26,309.88	6,526.20	3,32,836.08
178	3,32,836.08	6,656.72	3,39,492.80
179	3,39,492.80	6,789.86	3,46,282.66
180	3,46,282.66	6,925.65	3,53,208.31
181	3,53,208.31	7,064.17	3,60,272.48
182	3,60,272.48	7,205.45	3,67,477.93
183	3,67,477.93	7,349.56	3,74,827.49
184	3,74,827.49	7,496.55	3,82,324.04
185	3,82,324.04	7,646.48	3,89,970.52
186	3,89,970.52	7,799.41	3,97,769.93
187	3,97,769.93	7,955.40	4,05,725.33
188	4,05,725.33	8,114.50	4,13,839.83
189	4,13,839.83	8,276.80	4,22,116.63

Month	Initial Investment	2% Profit for the Whole Month	Balance at the End of the Month
190	4,22,116.63	8,442.33	4,30,558.96
191	4,30,558.96	8,611.18	4,39,170.14
192	4,39,170.14	8,783.41	4,47,953.55
193	4,47,953.55	8,959.07	4,56,912.62
194	4,56,912.62	9,138.25	4,66,050.87
195	4,66,050.87	9,321.02	4,75,371.89
196	4,75,371.89	9,507.43	4,84,879.32
197	4,84,879.32	9,697.59	4,94,576.91
198	4,94,576.91	9,891.54	5,04,468.45
199	5,04,468.45	10,089.37	5,14,557.82
200	5,14,557.82	10,291.15	5,24,848.97
201	5,24,848.97	10,496.98	5,35,345.95
202	5,35,345.95	10,706.92	5,46,052.87
203	5,46,052.87	10,921.06	5,56,973.93
204	5,56,973.93	11,139.48	5,68,113.41
205	5,68,113.41	11,362.27	5,79,475.68
206	5,79,475.68	11,589.51	5,91,065.19
207	5,91,065.19	11,821.30	6,02,886.49
208	6,02,886.49	12,057.73	6,1,4944.22

Month	Initial Investment	2% Profit for the Whole Month	Balance at the End of the Month
209	6,14,944.22	12,298.89	6,27,243.11
210	6,27,243.11	12,544.86	6,39,787.97
211	6,39,787.97	12,795.76	6,52,583.73
212	6,52,583.73	13,051.67	6,65,635.40
213	6,65,635.40	13,312.71	6,78,948.11
214	6,78,948.11	13,578.96	6,92,527.07
215	6,92,527.07	13,850.55	7,06,377.62
216	7,06,377.62	14,127.55	7,20,505.17
217	7,20,505.17	14,410.10	7,34,915.27
218	7,34,915.27	14,698.31	7,49,613.58
219	7,49,613.58	14,992.27	7,64,605.85
220	7,64,605.85	15,292.12	7,79,897.97
221	7,79,897.97	15,597.96	7,95,495.93
222	7,95,495.93	15,909.91	8,11,405.84
223	8,11,405.84	16,228.12	8,27,633.96
224	8,27,633.96	16,552.68	8,44,186.64
225	8,44,186.64	16,883.73	8,61,070.37
226	8,61,070.37	17,221.41	8,78,291.78
227	8,78,291.78	17,565.84	8,95,857.62

Month	Initial Investment	2% Profit for the Whole Month	Balance at the End of the Month
228	8,95,857.62	17,917.15	9,13,774.77
229	9,13,774.77	18,275.49	9,32,050.26
230	9,32,050.26	18,641.01	9,50,691.27
231	9,50,691.27	19,013.82	9,69,705.09
232	9,69,705.09	19,394.11	9,89,099.20
233	9,89,099.20	19,781.98	1,00,8881.18
234	10,08,881.18	20,177.65	10,29,058.80
235	10,29,058.80	20,581.18	10,49,639.98
236	10,49,639.98	20,992.80	10,70,632.78
237	10,70,632.78	21,412.66	10,92,045.43
238	10,92,045.43	21,840.91	11,13,886.34
239	11,13,886.34	22,277.73	11,36,164.07
240	11,36,164.07	22,723.28	11,58,887.35
241	11,58,887.35	23,177.75	11,82,065.10
242	11,82,065.10	23,641.30	12,05,706.40
243	12,05,706.40	24,114.13	12,29,820.53
244	12,29,820.53	24,596.41	12,54,416.94
245	12,54,416.94	25,088.34	12,79,505.28
246	12,79,505.28	25,590.10	13,05,095.38

Month	Initial Investment	2% Profit for the Whole Month	Balance at the End of the Month
247	13,05,095.38	26,101.91	13,31,197.29
248	13,31,197.29	26,623.95	13,57,821.24
249	13,57,821.24	27,156.42	13,84,977.66
250	13,84,977.66	27,699.55	14,12,677.21
251	14,12,677.21	28,253.55	14,40,930.76
252	14,40,930.76	28,818.61	14,69,749.37
253	14,69,749.37	29,394.99	14,99,144.36
254	14,99,144.36	29,982.89	15,29,127.25
255	15,29,127.25	30,582.54	15,59,709.79
256	15,59,709.79	31,194.20	15,90,903.99
257	15,90,903.99	31,818.08	16,22,722.07
258	16,22,722.07	32,454.44	16,55,176.51
259	16,55,176.51	33,103.53	16,88,280.04
260	16,88,280.04	33,765.60	17,22,045.64
261	17,22,045.64	34,440.92	17,56,486.56
262	17,56,486.56	35,129.73	17,91,616.29
263	17,91,616.29	35,832.32	18,27,448.61
264	18,27,448.61	36,548.97	18,63,997.58
265	18,63,997.58	37,279.96	19,01,277.54

Month	Initial Investment	2% Profit for the Whole Month	Balance at the End of the Month
266	19,01,277.54	38,025.55	19,39,303.09
267	19,39,303.09	38,786.06	19,78,089.15
268	19,78,089.15	39,561.78	20,17,650.93
269	20,17,650.93	40,353.02	20,58,003.95
270	20,58,003.95	41,160.08	20,99,164.03
271	20,99,164.03	41,983.28	21,41,147.31
272	21,41,147.31	42,822.95	21,83,970.26
273	21,83,970.26	43,679.40	22,27,649.66
274	22,27,649.66	44,552.99	22,72,202.65
275	22,72,202.65	45,444.06	23,17,646.71
276	23,17,646.71	46,352.93	23,63,999.64
277	23,63,999.64	47,279.99	24,11,279.63
278	24,11,279.63	48,225.60	24,59,505.23
279	24,59,505.23	49,190.10	25,08,695.33
280	25,08,695.33	50,173.91	25,58,869.24
281	25,58,869.24	51,177.38	26,10,046.62
282	26,10,046.62	52,200.94	26,62,247.56
283	26,62,247.56	53,244.95	27,15,492.51
284	27,15,492.51	54,309.85	27,69,802.36

Month	Initial Investment	2% Profit for the Whole Month	Balance at the End of the Month
285	27,69,802.36	55,396.04	28,25,198.40
286	28,25,198.40	56,503.97	28,81,702.37
287	28,81,702.37	57,634.05	29,39,336.42
288	29,39,336.42	58,786.73	29,98,123.15
289	29,98,123.15	59,962.46	30,58,085.61
290	30,58,085.61	61,161.71	31,19,247.32
291	31,19,247.32	62,384.95	31,81,632.27
292	31,81,632.27	63,632.64	32,45,264.91
293	32,45,264.91	64,905.30	33,10,170.21
294	33,10,170.21	66,203.41	33,76,373.62
295	33,76,373.62	67,527.47	34,43,901.09
296	34,43,901.09	68,878.02	35,12,779.11
297	35,12,779.11	70,255.58	35,83,034.69
298	35,83,034.69	71,660.70	36,54,695.39
299	36,54,695.39	73,093.90	37,27,789.29
300	37,27,789.29	74,555.79	38,02,345.08
301	38,02,345.08	76,046.90	38,78,391.98
302	38,78,391.98	77,567.84	39,55,959.82
303	39,55,959.82	79,119.20	40,35,079.02

Month	Initial Investment	2% Profit for the Whole Month	Balance at the End of the Month
304	40,35,079.02	80,701.58	41,15,780.60
305	41,15,780.60	82,315.61	41,98,096.21
306	41,98,096.21	83,961.92	42,82,058.13
307	42,82,058.13	85,641.17	43,67,699.30
308	43,67,699.30	87,353.98	44,55,053.28
309	44,55,053.28	89,101.07	45,44,154.35
310	45,44,154.35	90,883.09	46,35,037.44
311	46,35,037.44	92,700.74	47,27,738.18
312	47,27,738.18	94,554.77	48,22,292.95
313	48,22,292.95	96,445.86	49,18,738.81
314	49,18,738.81	98,374.77	50,17,113.58
315	50,17,113.58	1,00,342.28	51,17,455.86
316	51,17,455.86	1,02,349.11	52,19,804.97
317	52,19,804.97	1,04,396.10	53,24,201.07
318	53,24,201.07	1,06,484.02	54,30,685.09
319	54,30,685.09	1,08,613.71	55,39,298.80
320	55,39,298.80	1,10,785.97	56,50,084.77
321	56,50,084.77	1,1,3001.70	57,63,086.47
322	57,63,086.47	1,15,261.73	58,78,348.20

Month	Initial Investment	2% Profit for the Whole Month	Balance at the End of the Month
323	58,78,348.20	1,17,566.96	59,95,915.16
324	59,95,915.16	1,19,918.30	61,15,833.46
325	61,15,833.46	1,22,316.67	62,38,150.13
326	62,38,150.13	1,24,763.00	63,62,913.13
327	63,62,913.13	1,27,258.26	64,90,171.40
328	64,90,171.40	1,29,803.43	66,19,974.83
329	66,19,974.83	1,32,399.50	67,52,374.32
330	67,52,374.32	1,35,047.49	68,87,421.81
331	68,87,421.81	1,37,748.44	70,25,170.24
332	70,25,170.24	1,40,503.40	71,65,673.65
333	71,65,673.65	1,43,313.47	73,08,987.12
334	73,08,987.12	1,46,179.74	74,55,166.87
335	74,55,166.87	1,49,103.33	76,04,270.20
336	76,04,270.20	1,52,085.41	77,56,355.61
337	77,56,355.61	1,55,127.11	79,11,482.72
338	79,11,482.72	1,58,229.65	80,69,712.37
339	80,69,712.37	1,61,394.25	82,31,106.62
340	82,31,106.62	1,64,622.13	83,95,728.75
341	83,95,728.75	1,67,914.58	85,63,643.33

Month	Initial Investment	2% Profit for the Whole Month	Balance at the End of the Month
342	85,63,643.33	1,71,272.86	87,34,916.19
343	87,34,916.19	1,74,698.33	89,09,614.52
344	89,09,614.52	1,78,192.29	90,87,806.81
345	90,87,806.81	1,81,756.13	92,69,562.94
346	92,69,562.94	1,85,391.26	94,54,954.20
347	94,54,954.20	1,89,099.09	96,44,053.29
348	96,44,053.29	1,92,881.06	98,36,934.35
349	98,36,934.35	1,96,738.69	1,00,33,673.04
350	1,00,33,673.04	2,00,673.46	1,02,34,346.50
351	1,02,34,346.50	2,04,686.93	1,04,39,033.43
352	1,04,39,033.43	2,08,780.67	1,06,47,814.10
353	1,06,47,814.10	2,12,956.28	1,08,60,770.38
354	1,08,60,770.38	2,17,215.41	1,10,77,985.79
355	1,10,77,985.79	2,21,559.72	1,12,99,545.51
356	1,12,99,545.51	2,25,990.91	1,15,25,536.42
357	1,15,25,536.42	2,30,510.72	1,17,56,047.14
358	1,17,56,047.14	2,35,120.95	1,19,91,168.09
359	1,19,91,168.09	2,39,823.36	1,22,30,991.45
360	1,22,30,991.45	2,44,619.83	1,24,75,611.28

□□□